Aestas

2015

Edited By
Anirban Ray Choudhury

Cover Art: Anisha Bhaduri
Cover Design: Anirban Ray Choudhury

Published by Fabula Press in January 2016

First Edition

www.fabulapress.com

ISBN-10: 1523728264
ISBN-13: 978-1523728268

CONTENTS

Foreword

1 Saint Kizito   1

2 The Luft Mensch   23

3 Summer Skin   41

4 How Do You Know   51

5 Dear Violet   75

6 Last Prayers at the Chapel   85

7 First Kill   101

8 Flower Behind Her Ear   113

9 Something Else Happened   129

10 Long John of Babylon   145

11 The Loudest Laugh of All   157

12 The Mart   177

13 White Wings   191

14 Dragon Bird of Liaoning   205

About the Judges   223

About the Editor   229

ACKNOWLEDGMENTS

We thank Anisha, Brett, Clare and Leela for agreeing to sit in as judges, and for their professional feedback on the stories and the contest format. This book would not have been possible without their support. We also remain deeply indebted to our patrons; and to the little known authors who are keeping the art of the short story alive.

FOREWORD

We usher in 2016 with yet another edition of the Aestas anthology. As always, it was a tremendously satisfying reading season with some glorious tales making their way to our desks through the Aestas contest. And as always, at the end we were left wondering if the next anthology will be able to surpass, or even be as good as, Aestas 2015. Yes, whether there are enough writers of calibre taking an interest in weaving together the more concise form of the fable remains a constant worry for us. It is not an unfounded worry; with little by way of monetary compensation, the charm of short stories fast loses its sheen for the budding writer who prefers to set his sights on something bigger - the big N. Justifiably so, because a short story is essentially a work of art, but rarely the means to the end a writer so desperately seeks; barring a few exceptions (a la' Jhumpa Lahiri), short stories seldom bring the recognition and riches that a novel has to offer.

The digital publishing era has made the waters even murkier, and the survival of the short story is now being threatened more than ever. Back in the days when there were only print publications, letters from the readers to these publications often served as critiques for stories, highlighting the writers' strengths and weaknesses. The readers decided what they wanted to read, and authors had to develop their style accordingly or find their own niche coterie of readers. The tables have since turned; thanks to the option of self publishing many writers are blindly churning out novels (sometimes as many as five or six a year), hoping to lure readers by sheer numbers. The industry is also seeing more and more paid book reviewers jumping in for a piece of the pie, and whilst many of them work with integrity (e.g. Kirkus Reviews), more often than not the author ends up spending more on getting the book out in front of the readers than can be made from self publishing royalties. There are a few success stories, of course, but these remain few and far between. For most it is more about wasted resources, resources that could have been better utilized honing the only skill really required in this industry – the ability to write, and write well.

Not everything is gloomy, though. We still see new magazines and periodicals cropping up, and more often than not the digital platform provides a good opportunity for such ventures, whether be it for generating publicity for a print publication or for hosting an online magazine. I feel particularly elated when there are new publications, for those that manage to survive in this extremely competitive and often cruel environment herald new hope for literature in general, and its shorter form in particular.

The past year also saw quite a few such publications surface, and I am quite hopeful about two new venues for the short story – Christopher Fielden's annual contest anthology "To Hull and Back", and the Danilo Kis inspired Hourglass Literary Magazine. The former is in its third year now but really came into the reckoning in 2015, and is run by the man whom most short story writers know as the librarian of contest listings (see http://www.christopherfielden.com). The latter is a true-blue newbie, a fresh bi-lingual magazine being run from Bosnia with Vojislav Voki Erceg at the helm of affairs. The "To Hull and Back" contest is run on a not-for-profit model, and receives some marvelous submissions - the latest anthology is a case in point carrying some really great stories. Hourglass on the other hand is yet to come out with their first collection which is due this year, and yours truly is looking forward to reading some delightful fiction as guest editor.

Closer home, at Fabula Press we also saw some really amazing writing with Aestas 2015, and personally speaking I found it rather painful to turn down some of the stories. In many cases it was a matter of logistics; we were constrained to make choices between stories with similar themes, or in a few instances even base our judgement on the number of past publishing credits where we aim to have a few fresh voices in every collection.

That's all from me for now. As always, bouquets/brickbats are welcome at editors@fabulapress.com, and we will certainly appreciate honest feedback on Amazon/Goodreads and the like.

~ Anirban

Aestas 2015

Saint Kizito
Caroline Mbaya

Caroline Kinya Mbaya grew up in a small town on the Kenyan highlands. She is currently an economics professor in Barcelona Spain and writes fiction in her spare time. Her work has been shortlisted in *Wasafiri New Writing Prize* and long listed in *Fish Short Story contest* and *The Short Fiction Prize*. She is working on her first collection of short stories.

In the deeply humane and moving *Saint Kizito*, Caroline explores a gruesome incident at a boarding school in Kenya in 1991, skillfully tying together the lives of the victims and the vanquished. Judge Brett Sanders is ecstatic as he says *"The expert weaving of a complex plot, foreground and back-story together with the picture-perfect characterizations, especially of the two strong women whose journey this really is, took my breath away."*

23.45 Hrs, Maua Maximum Prison

Meeme craned his neck when he heard approaching footsteps. From the gap under his metal cell door he could see the shadow of the advancing night guard grow shorter. Soon it would grow longer again as the guard completed the night patrol and went towards the light at the exit that illuminated the entire cell block. The guard's footsteps were slow and heavy, accompanied by raspy breathing and an occasional wheeze. Meeme estimated that it was a quarter to midnight. The prisoners had come to learn how to tell the time depending on which guard was doing the patrol. The oldest guard at the prison had the midnight shift.

Meeme gave the signal to the other seven men in his cell. Just minutes before, all eight of them had been down under the crack next to the wall, scraping out dirt with their bare hands. Now they lay down on their mattresses and covered themselves with a single blanket that acted as their sole source of warmth. Lying there under the blanket, the stench from the shit bucket was magnified. His oldest friend Kungu's nervousness had revealed itself through diarrhoea and the whole cell stank of rotten eggs and dead rats. During their prison life, Kungu was the one among them who managed to maintain a chubby figure, thanks mainly to his having been stationed as a prison cook. Meeme who languished under the hard labour section, lifting stones and tilling dry land, had grown stooped and wiry.

Meeme saw the guard's flashlight pass through their cell, resting on each of the eight mounds under the blanket.

"Two, three, four...

Wheeze

Cough

...seven eight"

Meeme lay on the thin mattress waiting for the guard's shadow to grow longer; his thoughts veering to another midnight in a time long past, a midnight that had so unalterably changed the course of his life.

And although now, just like then, he had been the one to give the signal to the others waiting in the shadows, he told himself that this time was different. This time there was no recklessness. He was a reformed man.

A man who had paid for his sins. It was time to start a new life. He thought about his younger brother waiting for him outside the prison walls. It had been agreed that he wait with a donkey cart filled with napier grass below the drain pipes where they would emerge. His heart felt heavy. His brother was the only member of his family who had visited him in prison every year in the last 24 years.

Aaarrgggg

Kungu groaned. The guard who had been retreating to the exit shuffled back to cell one and flashed his light one more time. Meeme buried his head in the torn mattress, and wondered if they should leave Kungu and his nervousness behind. He would no doubt get them caught if the police dogs followed the smell of his diarrhoearing arse.

Finally, after what seemed like two drought seasons, the night guard's footsteps retreated and a noisy lock clicked in the distance. Beneath the pongy blanket, eight heads came up for air, eight pairs of eyes searching each other in the darkness. Meeme nodded to the men staring at him. It was time.

00.30. Hrs, Maua Mental hospital

Ntiboka sat in the brightly lit common room with knitting needles tugging at two balls of wool. She was trying to finish a yellow and grey sweater, a present for her sister's daughter. She kept looking out for the nurse who came around to give them their medicines. She knew that once she took the medicine she would be groggy. Her hands would become numb and she would need to lie down. She was determined to finish the sweater before the Sunday visit which was three days away.

Sister Geovana, the new Consolata sister who worked with them at the workshop had been teaching her knitting patterns. Cats. Owls. Stars. Now her knitting had started to look like the pictures in the Italian magazines that Sister Geovana brought to the workshop.

Ntiboka felt happier since she started knitting again. She felt useful. Once she started she just couldn't stop. She had knitted a sweater for her father, her mother, her three brothers and their children, and now she was knitting for her sister's daughter who having turned three had stopped being scared to come and visit her at the hospital. These days she was in a better place, not like in the years before Sister Geovana came. That time all she could see were images of that midnight. The night of dying bodies next to her and of boys genitals pounding on her. She closed her eyes and shook her head.

She recited Sister Geovana's mantra. "Happy thoughts, only happy thoughts."

Ntiboka looked up at the wall clock next to the zebra print curtains. Nurse was never late with the medicine. Dark shadows had started descending from the bare walls and were now turning into a screaming mob. They started approaching her. Ntiboka got up and put her knitting needles in the drawer with her name on it. She straightened her white cotton gown and sunk her cold feet into soft woollen slippers.

It was August, the hottest month of the year with scorching days and freezing nights. Ntiboka felt light-headed as she made her way to the nurses' room so she walked next to the wall to support herself on the oil-painted blue wall. She noticed for the first time that the common room was virtually abandoned. When she got to the nurses room at the end of the corridor she found the patients and nurses huddled around the television set. She went over and tapped Nurse on the shoulder.

"*Imbi?*"

Nurse frowned. "Speak English Ntiboka, not Kimeru. That way everyone can understand you. Ask me again"

"What going on nurse?"

"Very good. Now, it seems some prisoners from Maua Prison escaped about thirty minutes ago.

"*Keke!*"

Ntiboka saw that Nurse was about to admonish her again but now she was more afraid of the faces on the television. One of the faces resembled a shadow that had been lurking on the walls, which were now jumping on her. She waved her hands frantically to fight them off and started to wail.

She heard Nurse's voice "Come. Ntiboka, let me give you your medicine."

Ntiboka shook her head and sat on the floor, rocking herself back and forth her head buried in her knees.

Nurse rushed off to the direction of the medicine cabinet. When she got back five minutes later patient Ntiboka M'Mwirithia could not be found.

00.45 Hrs, Maua Police station

Sergeant Gatwiri walked into her office, locked the door, and turned on the radio. Her favourite station was playing some noisy Lingala music. The sounds of bass guitar and drums would provide the much needed distraction. She got behind her desk, a wide grey metal desk with matching cabinets, and sat on the wooden chair and tilted her head towards the ceiling. She fought back tears. She hated it when she got this way.

Her eyes darted around the small office in the remote police post. The picture of the president, hung on old termite infested planks of wood that walled the station, stared down at her. Right next to it was her certificate of rank. She turned her head towards the navy blue metal door. Her police cap still lay where she had left it; on top of the dusty wooden cabinet filled with trophies that had faded with time.

Thirty minutes earlier, she had taken off her white police cap and dark-blue jacket and left them in her office (to give the impression that she was in the vicinity). Then she had gone anxiously to Bariu's office as she had done every night they had been on duty together for the last three weeks. She sat on his metal desk, lifted her blue skirt and let his long sinewy fingers climb up to her moistness. After they were done, she sat in a chair by the corner panting, despising him then herself, feeling released then feeling dirty.

During the day when she ran into him at the station, she noticed his big eyes undressing her; from the curly hair that sat under an oversized cap, to the white collar that stood in contrast to her dark-tar skin down to the breast pockets on her blue jacket where her badges were pinned then to the bulging midsection where two pregnancies had left their mark and finally down to the curve of her hips where her blue skirt hugged her tightly. She would catch him watching her, licking his lips and cracking his long fingers and her body would ache with longing. She would count the hours when she would finally be alone with him.

But when they were finally done and the heat was out her body, she cursed herself for being so needy. Bariu was her junior officer and word of their affair would have them both expelled. She thought about her husband, who since he had been discharged from the military almost a year back, had taken to alcohol as his staple diet and was no longer tending to her needs. He had started to suspect something was amiss since she was now arriving home late quite often.

She opened her top drawer and took out the picture of her husband and children. Her two little boys were smiling widely at her. Divorce was out of the question. The boys needed their father. She had to stop risking her marriage like this. She got up, wiped her face and put on her cap, then her jacket and sat back down. She started to close the drawer when she noticed that her mobile phone, lying next to the picture frame, had over twenty missed calls.

Had something happened to the children? Had her husband been found dead in a ditch? It was unusual for her sister-in-law to call her so late.

"Nancy? You called?" she queried when her sister-in-law finally picked up.

"Gatwiri, where have you been? Gosh! I've called you like a million times, *mwana.*"

"Yes I've seen. Police work. *Imbi? Imbi?*"

"Ntiboka is missing, they called from the hospital just a

few minutes ago. They can't find her."

"Your sister? I thought you said she was getting better."

"She was. But I'm really worried about her whereabouts, especially now that there are prisoners on the loose-"

"Prisoners on the loose? What do—."

Just then there was loud banging on Sergeant Gatwiri's door.

"I'll call you back Nancy."

Sergeant Gatwiri knew the only person who banged on her door that way was her superior, the Chief Inspector. She straightened her uniform before opening the door.

"Sergeant Gatwiri!"

"Chief Inspector!" Sergeant Gatwiri stood as straight as a pole and made a quick salute.

"I've been trying to reach you for the last hour. Where have you been?"

"In the evidence room sir! We retrieved some AK 47s from cattle rustlers from Tharaka and I was filing the evidence." She responded trying not to meet his eyes.

"And Officer Bariu? Isn't he on duty? Anyway, some prisoners dug their way out of Maua Maximum prison this evening. I need all the men I can for a manhunt. Here's the list of the escaped convicts."

Sergeant Gatwiri went over the list. One of the men's names jumped at her. Ntiboka's disappearance was not a random occurrence.

01.00 hrs

"Keep your head down Meeme! There's another police car approaching us." Meeme's brother hissed under his breath. He was at the front of the donkey cart while eight men were buried under napier grass behind. Meeme's heart beat like a war drum. Every time lights washed over the cart, he saw himself back in that rat-hole he had called home for over two decades.

They were on the highway, heading one kilometre down to an abandoned tea factory that Kungu's family owned. The men could hear dogs barking in the distance and voices calling out to one another. They knew that news of their escape had probably reached their families by now. It was a good thing that they had decided to make their getaway in a donkey cart. No one would suspect a drunkard with a cart full of napier grass singing loudly about his love for a barmaid.

The cart rocked from side to side on the pot-holed tarmac road. Meeme's brother sang louder. They wondered if he was still pretending to be drunk or if he had actually imbibed to get courage.

"*Simama*!"

The cart came to an abrupt stop. They held their breaths. The men heard Meeme's brother disembark and shuffle his feet to where the order had come from.

"Hey! You're drunk and still transporting cow grass at this time of the night?" they heard a man ask in Swahili.

"N-n-no officerrrr."

The men buried under napier heard two pairs of footsteps around the cart. They felt a hand rummaging above them and they sank deeper into the grass. They all held their breaths, even Kungu who had been panting like a dog since they emerged from the prison drainage pipes.

Finally the man said, "Go home. There are dangerous criminals on the loose tonight."

"Yesssh sir."

"*Aa*! And this local brew will finish these young men *bwana*," the officer finally said and some men with him laughed in response.

Meeme's brother boarded the cart, cracked a whip and the donkeys started suddenly. The men were thrown up then down then against each other as the cart continued to gain speed every time the whip cracked. He was no longer singing. The seriousness of aiding escaped convicts seemed to have hit him just then and he was in a hurry to get it over and done with.

After a few minutes, they felt the cart turn into a rough road and slope towards the front. The men slid downwards and bumped into each other again. Meeme heard Kungu let out a sigh of relief and knew that they were on the final stretch down to the river bank. He lifted his head out of the napier grass and smiled. The abandoned building, illuminated by a full moon stood just meters ahead. It overlooked the Maua River and was where Kungu and Meeme had spent most of their childhood; running through tea bushes, hiding under the tea trucks and diving into the clear river for fish. The building had fallen to ruin when tea farming was replaced by *Miraa*, Khat. Their much loved stimulant. These days, the river had blackened from sewage and industrial waste and the building housed only mice and squirrels. The cart slowed down and came to a stop. Meeme's brother jumped off. The other men started to hoist themselves out but he held up a hand.

"Wait!"

The men heard a truck engine in the distance; the boisterous sound seemed to be coming towards them, growing closer and closer. Just as they were about to disembark and start running towards the river, the engine roar started to fade and they listened as it grew distant until finally only the torrent of the water below and chirping of crickets interrupted the quiet night.

Meeme's brother circled the building and went inside. He came out and signalled. The eight men in beige uniforms followed him wordlessly. Inside he pointed them to a corner where a kerosene lamp was flickering. Next to it were loaves of bread, a tea-flask, cigarettes and some bundles of *Miraa* wrapped in banana stalk. He went back out and returned with a bag of old clothes and some hats. The men took turns undressing and stuffing buttered bread into their mouths.

Less than ten minutes later, the men emerged all dressed up in farmers clothing and carrying hoes. With the exception of Meeme and Kungu, the men had planned to sleep on top of the trees in the *Miraa* plantations and mix with the first shift of farmers that started collecting *Miraa* at four in the morning. They had agreed that it was safer for each man to make his own arrangements once they arrived at the old factory.

The men clapped each other on the back and hugged tightly. They knew that this was probably the last time they would meet. They had known each other in prison for most of their adult lives. Kungu and Meeme stood and watched as their former cell mates dispersed in different directions. They watched as the bodies turned into shadows, growing smaller as they moved into the plains littered with shrubs and long strands of grass swaying in the wind. Soon the shadows became one with the trees and the remaining men went back into the building and embraced.

"A new beginning, brother!"

"Yes, Meeme, we have paid our dues."

Meeme's brother came back in smelling of kerosene. Kungu lit a cigarette and picked some *Miraa* sticks from a bundle and started chewing then walked to another door-less room and left the brothers to talk.

"How's Maami? And Baaba?" Meeme turned to his younger brother now that they were alone. He wanted to tell him how grateful he was that he had risked his life for him. But he found himself asking about their parents instead. Maybe it was because they hadn't been to see him once since he had been imprisoned. Were they still angry at him?

"They died, Meeme. Two years after you went to prison, Baaba died of depression and Maami followed soon after. I didn't finish primary school. I had to take care of our two younger sisters."

Meeme turned away. He could feel hot salty tears stinging his eyes. His brother, three years younger, had been twelve when he was arrested. Why had his brother not said anything during his annual visits? Why did he make it look like everything was alright?

"And you have you married? Do you have children?"

His brother was silent.

"Meeme, what do you plan to do now that you're out?"

"*Heh?* I ask you a question and you answer me with a question. *Heh?*"

11

"Do you ever think about how your actions affected us? Which woman wants to marry the brother of a rapist, a murderer?"

"Brother, forgive me. We were young. It was a long time ago."

"Well, our lives have never been the same since then. Anyway, I need to return the donkey cart I leased. I'll bring you food and money in the morning. It would be safer if you to leave for Nairobi at first light. I'm sure they will launch a man-hunt along the river tomorrow."

Meeme's brother got up walked out of the building. Meeme wanted to grab his hand and embrace him. He wanted to be the big brother his siblings had once looked up to. But the years of separation between them ran deep like a river that had eaten its way through stone and formed two cliffs. The donkey cart crawled back up the hill. Meeme stood outside watching; shielding himself from the glow of the full moon against the pillars. He walked down a few rocky steps and sat in the darkness near the river. His tears flowed freely. He stared down at his rippled reflection in the dark river that resembled a mass of tar. The pungent monstrosity staring back terrified him. It seemed like just yesterday when the river was clear as day.

Through his tears, he saw his younger self emerge from the river naked holding a spear in his hand at the end of which was a small fish. The sky was clear and he squinted to avoid the strong glare of the sun against his water drenched eyelids.

"Look what I caught Ntiboka! Lo-oo-ok!" he said to a honey-skinned girl with long dark plaits sitting on the rocks above him in a yellow petticoat.

"*Phuuu*, that's a very small fish for your big sto-ma-ch," she teased back.

"Who did you just call big stomach? *heh*?" he started to run after her. But his chunky frame was no match for the light as deer girl running and squealing in laughter.

He loved the sound of her giggles as he raced after her but he wished she would not humiliate him by running so fast. She was a girl after all. They were supposed to let the boys win.

12

"Ntiboka! Come back here. You know I'll catch you eventually!" He had difficulty manoeuvring the rocks in the river and by the time he caught up with her, he would be out of breath, and his insides would be boiling over. He wished he was lean and good looking like his friend Kungu who just had the right amount of fat to reflect his family's affluence. Patrick Lumumba and Nelson Mandela were not obese. Che Guevara was not overweight. He needed to re-invent his image. His uncle's political science books had shown him as much.

Sounds of footsteps along the river startled Meeme and images of his childhood quickly faded away into the night. He got up cautiously and craned his neck. He turned his gaze upwards towards the building and saw Kungu watching him. It was probably a squirrel. No one would be around these parts at this time of night. He stared back into the river where the girl from his memories had been sitting and speculated if he should try and find her. Sometimes in prison he had wondered how she was doing. He guessed she was married by now and tried to imagine what her children would look like.

He shook his head, as if to dust off his memories, blew his nose between his thumb and forefinger and wiped his hand on a bush nearby then went back into the building.

The full moon shone on a woman walking in zig-zag motion by the river. She saw six shadows disperse into the shrubs above. Two shadows remained behind and walked into a large building. One shadow was pouring some liquid in a large tin container and throwing clothes inside. Soon the container was on fire and the shadow went back into the building.

She sat on a rock overlooking the building and watched. Her feet ached. She couldn't tell how long she had been running. She hadn't been here for years but her legs seemed to have memorised the path that wove through farms of napier grass and *Miraa* trees. This was where she had fallen in love, where she lay when a man first took her.

After a few minutes she saw a shadow emerging from the house and she crouched behind the rock. Then she saw the shadow get on a donkey cart and go up the hill. On impulse, the woman got up and made her way towards the building.

For thirty minutes since she had heard of the prison break, and after she had watched the Chief Inspector drive off in an old government Land Rover, Sergeant Gatwiri had gone around barking orders and receiving radio updates from various police search parties. She had been in a state of indecision since she saw his name on the list. She was surprised that a man she had loved as a girl still tugged the strings to her heart.

The Chief Inspector called her on the radio.

"Sergeant Gatwiri! What have you gathered about the suspects? Over! "

"I recognise one of the prisoners names, sir! I suspect he was the ring leader during the St. Kizito Genocide. Over!"

"Are you sure? We need to know the nature of their crimes so that we can attest if they are armed and dangerous. Over!"

"I have that case file in storage. I'll retrieve it and inform you right away. Over!"

"Radio me as soon as you can. I've asked the Kaithe and Meru police stations to erect roadblocks on the Meru-Maua highway. The media will be all over this in the morning, Sergeant. We need to move fast! Over."

"Yes sir! Over and out!"

Sergeant Gatwiri retrieved a bunch of keys from the front desk officer and headed across the yard where the old police post stood. She tried to imagine where the men would hide once they got out. She needed to find them before the search parties did. It was the only way to keep Kungu safe. As the old shipping container that held closed cases came to view, Sergeant Gatwiri realised that she had forgotten to bring a kerosene lamp.

"*Mai*!" she cursed.

14

Officer Bariu emerged from the shadows. "Take it easy I have a flashlight." She couldn't see him clearly but she knew he was wearing a smirk on his face. He enjoyed making her nervous. Probably because of his twisted idea that a woman was not fit to be his boss. He flashed the light on the large padlock as she started trying the keys on the lock. Her hands were shaking. It had been a long time since she had thought about that last night at St. Kizito.

"So what were you and the Chief up to in your office?" Officer Bariu growled, lighting a cigarette and blowing smoke in her face. He was taunting her. But she was in no mood for it. A door from her past had opened and ghosts were rushing through.

Finally she got the padlock open and pushed the metal door. She grabbed the flashlight from Officer Bariu and started scanning the shelves. Officer Bariu straightened up and put out his cigarette. He eyed her cautiously.

"What year are we looking for Sergeant?"

"1991."

Sergeant Gatwiri found the file almost immediately. The rest of the files were usually two or three pages, but the St.Kizito case file, filled with evidence reports, pictures of suspects and press cuttings, and with an accused list of more than twenty, was one of the bulkiest.

"I'll need to take this back to the office and go through it. Thanks for the flashlight officer."

"*Keke!* Gatwiri , do you want to talk about it? You don't normally get this affected by cases. "

She spun around.

"*Ser-gea-nt!* Ok *afande?* Take the van and join the others at the manhunt!"

She marched back to her office, locked the door and spread out the contents of the file on her desk. The headshot of a smiling good-looking boy stood out right away. She swallowed hard. *Kungu Mwebia*, the name under the picture read. Had he been smiling when they took his picture at the police station? Had he not even contemplated the heinous crime they had committed?

How could she have been so wrong about him? How could she have planned to spend her life with this boy?

She leafed through the pictures; faces of boys stared back at her. Boys who had laughed with her in the dining hall, who had helped her with her chemistry assignment, the picture of the school prankster, the picture of a boy who had rushed her to hospital in his father's car- all looking back at her with that same look that made her wonder if they hadn't all been drunk on sugar-cane beer that night.

Then the picture of her nemesis appeared. *Meeme Justus.* The boy who had planned it all. The boy who had turned her Kungu into an extremist. It was Meeme she wanted dead.

A press report caught her eye. She picked it up and sat down to read.

July 1991, St.Kizito Mixed High School, Maua

By Nation Correspondent.

In the High school named after the youngest Ugandan Martyr, the dormitory is a time capsule: July 13, 1991.

Everything remains as it was the morning after the slayings. Bodies have been removed, but the bunk beds lie in twisted heaps. Suitcases and clothes are strewn around the room. Several pairs of torn and bloody underwear lie on the floor.

Over 70 girls were raped and 19 killed at St. Kizito Mixed High School. The chaos began after the girls supposedly declined to participate in a strike organized by the boys at the school. Once the boys cut the power, they began screaming and throwing rocks at the girls' dorms that were made of cinder block and tin roofs. The 271 girls of St. Kizito crammed themselves into one dormitory. As the boys battered the door in an attempt to get to them, the girls rushed to the far corner of the room. The door gave way and the boys descended on them. Several teachers who board at the school could have stopped it, but were too terrified of the 306 male students. Two night watchmen, armed with bows and arrows, did not attempt to stop the assault on the girls'. By 3:30, Maua hospital was overflowing with injured girls.

Police discovered the bodies piled atop one another and autopsies showed that none of the dead had been raped. They had been crushed to death in the stampede to escape. Twenty-nine St. Kizito boys are being held without bail on manslaughter charges.

Some of the girls interviewed claimed that rape in school was common and usually went unreported. "A boy drags you into the bushes and has his way with you. You take it and hope not to fall pregnant," one of the girls explained, a fact echoed by many locals who felt that if girls had not died, the incident may have never made the news.

Others believe that a school named after the 14 year-old boy Saint, burned alive for his Christian beliefs, was bound to bring a bad omen. The school has been temporarily closed down and the remaining students transferred. When it re-opens its gates next year, it will go under a different name.

Sergeant Gatwiri started to cry, softly at first, but soon her chest was heaving in sobs. It seemed like just yesterday that she was sixteen, when the older girls at the school had used their bodies to barricade the door so that the younger girls could escape through the window.

Even now she kept wondering how it had all gone wrong on that Friday evening. The boys who were their brothers, who had loved them, had turned against them like a pack of hyenas.

She picked a dated picture of an old school assembly, with the Kenyan flag displayed on the flag post. Voices started floating back to her; the old conversations came to life.

"Gatwiri you need to talk to the other girls and convince them! You're the class prefect."

"Kungu, stop being a radical. Us girls are not going to strike because you boys say so."

"Listen to me. This thing is serious. The boys are not happy that the headmaster won't let us attend the High school sporting tournament."

"So what Kungu? *Heh*? We have exams to study for anyway."

" *Aiiiii!* I knew there was no point trying to explain these things to a woman!"

"Kungu! That boy you're hanging out with these days is poisoning your mind!"

"*Wewe*! Don't say such things. Meeme is a visionary!"

"Yeah? Is that why he is constantly getting expelled?"

"There you go again, sounding smart. I'm warning you, the boys don't like being mocked. If you don't do as we say we'll teach you girls a lesson."

Gatwiri was silent. She had never seen Kungu in this state of lunacy before. He came from one of the well-off families in Maua and had led a sheltered life. She decided to take a different approach. She held his hand and smiled coyly.

"*Ai*. Don't say such things. Hey, why don't we get away this evening to your Baaba's factory at the river? I'll skip prep and get someone to cover for me. Wait until you see what I've got for you."

He yanked his hand away.

"Leave me alone! Today is the day when real men must prove themselves."

And with that, he walked away leaving Gatwiri with a puzzled expression on her face. His outburst had startled her. Once or twice she had heard that a boy in school had been violent with one of the girls, but no one ever reported it. She increased her pace and went looking for her best friend. She found her at the school canteen talking to a man in military uniform.

She called out, "Nancy!"

18

Nancy turned and gestured to her to come over.

"Gatwiri this is my big brother, he just got recruited into the army," Nancy said to her of the well groomed young man in green khaki uniform seated next to her with a box of army provisions.

Gatwiri smiled politely and shook his extended hand. Nancy had been trying to set them up for a while.

She said to him, still forcing a smile, "Sorry to take away your sister but the head teacher requires us right away."

Nancy seemed surprised. "Yes? Why it's only mid-day, normally we are not required until half past one."

Gatwiri stood at a distance as her friend saw her brother off.

When she caught up with her Nancy said, "Hey, what's going on?"

"Nancy I have a bad feeling about something."

"What? What? Tell me!"

"I think your sister's boyfriend is inciting the boys."

Nancy laughed. "Who? Meeme? That fatty-fatty boy?"

"I'm serious. Some of the boys act like he's their Mandela or something. Just now Kungu was talking about teaching the girls a lesson if we don't join in the strike."

"Do you think they can really do it? Hurt us I mean?"

"Who knows? Isn't that how mob psychology works?"

"Gatwiri, leave that Kungu alone. So what did you think of my brother anyway? *Heh*? Fresh? *Heh*?"

Gatwiri was too preoccupied with the strange feeling of impending doom.

"Don't you remember last term when that Meeme boy encouraged everyone to trash the dining hall because they served us *Ugali* made of yellow maize flour? I think we should report it to the headmaster."

"*Wewe!* What if you get Kungu in trouble, all for nothing? Maybe he was just blowing steam. But if you report him he could be expelled."

Gatwiri was silent. Nancy was right. Maybe it was just talk.

Later that night, at around nine in the evening when the lights went off she made nothing of it. Power outages were common and the girls usually went to their dorms early in the case of a blackout. However a few minutes later when they heard loud bangs on the dormitories' roof, Gatwiri knew that the boys were carrying out their threat.

A knock on her door brought her back.

"Yes?"

The desk officer walked in and saluted.

"Sergeant, news from the field is that three escapees have been caught on the upper side of river Maua."

Sergeant Gatwiri stopped to think for a moment. *Of course. Our old hideout. The abandoned factory.*

"Thank-you officer."

Sergeant Gatwiri grabbed the car keys from her cabinet and ran out. She wondered how she would feel seeing Kungu after all this time. Memories of him over the years had been clouded by accusing faces of her dying schoolmates. Faces that had pushed her into the police academy, their cries for help had been the driving force every time she almost gave up and quit the force. She would never be helpless gain. The guilt of getting away unhurt while so many others perished had been like the devil chasing her tail.

She started the old police Landover. It choked and sputtered a few times before it roared to life and she sped down the highway.

02.00Hrs

Ntiboka sat in the darkness watching Meeme sleep. He was lying on his stomach with one arm outstretched. Next to him a man also slept, lying on his back in a contorted position as if his arms and legs couldn't agree on a direction to face. She knew they would not wake up.

She looked at her hands; they were red and sticky, like when Sister Geovana made them work with clay. Her white dress was also drenched in a sticky substance.

Meeme had been surprised to see her when she came upon him with a rock. She wondered why he hadn't tried to fight back. He just stood there as she hit him over and over until the insides of his head were pouring out on her dress.

The man sleeping next to Meeme had tried to stop her. He had tried to grab her by the waist as Meeme fell to the ground. She heard the man calling her name. How did he know her name? Was he one of the shadows? She turned on him with a rusty tea-shaving blade.

That night so many years ago she had tried to fight back. But she had been too weak, too scared. And for years after that she had been battling with the shadows. In her dreams. On the walls of the hospital. In her room as she lay on her bed. Now as the men's groans grew quiet, she felt the haze lifting. A car pulled up outside and footsteps ran towards her. Ntiboka sat in foetal position. She was no longer afraid.

The footsteps came closer and she picked up the bloodied blade. A woman's voice called out to her.

"Ntiboka! Is that you, Ntiboka? What have you done?"

Through a crack on the wall, the moon shone a light on the approaching woman wearing a police uniform. Ntiboka smiled. Her sister's friend.

The two women looked at each other, then at the men lying in a pool of blood.

Her sister's friend knelt over the man next to Meeme and started to cry. Then she got up and put the bloodied blade into a plastic bag, went outside and threw it into the river below. She came back and held out a hand to her.

"Let's go home."

***

The Luft Mensch
Peter Newall

Peter Newall lives in Sydney, Australia, but spends the northern winters travelling by train through the border cities of Central and Eastern Europe, pursuing the ghosts of the Habsburg Empire and the former Soviet Union and learning German and Russian. From 2011 to 2013 he lived in Odessa, Ukraine, where he led a popular blues band. The city has left a mark on him, as *The Luft Mensch* does for us. Judge Anisha says of this story "A good story warms you. A great story keeps one awake at night. In a great story, the transference – of the plot, subplots, characters, atmosphere – is so complete that readers cannot stop asking themselves why and then, why not. This is a debate that builds up a noise that is so resonant, so desolate, so full of promise that one wants to stay up the night to listen to it, to resolve it, to conquer the mind of the writer. The Luft Mensch kept me awake. Needless to say, it is a great story."

The tram pulled in to the terminus, hissed, and came to a halt. Jerkily unfolding its segmented doors, it began to disgorge the crowd of passengers that had packed inside along its route, more at each stop. The last had been a group of students from the Polytechnic who jammed into the already-crowded carriage with wet boots, coats and rucksacks.

Yashe was not in a hurry. He let the students get out first, then, fastening his coat, climbed down the metal steps and walked watchfully across the tram tracks. There were still patches of ice between the muddy paths trodden across the uneven ground, and it was slippery underfoot.

As he was stepping over the low chain fence onto the footpath, a departing tram came round the corner. The driver pressed the electric bell. Its sudden loud shrilling made Yashe jump. He scrambled over the fence and turned, out of a sense of self-protection, to face the tram as it went by; as it passed him its wheels screamed on the curving metal rails. Along the blue sides of the tramcar parallel streaks of dirty orange ran downwards from rusted rivets. It looked roughly made, like something beaten into the approximate shape of a tram and sent out in haste to carry workers to the factory. He watched the glow of its red tail-light in the damp white air as it pulled away. Then, hunching his shoulders, he turned down the cracked asphalt footpath toward the park.

As he walked past the row of small prefabricated shops that served the tram terminus, a teenage boy in uniform, with the haircut of a first-year conscript, came out of one of them. He stared at Yashe aggressively, turning his head to maintain the stare as Yashe passed him. Yashe felt the eyes on the back of his neck for a good ten paces as he walked on, but he reached the park without the solider taking a step toward him.

The park was bordered with dark pine trees. Above their pointed tops, the sky was a dirty greyish-white, not any colour he could name. It was stretched out like a bedsheet, without any feature to give it depth or perspective. The dull flat sky made the gold domes of Saint Panteleimon's church appear two-dimensional, like the background to an icon.

It was darker under the pines, and he could smell their astringent needles crushed underfoot on the path. The rain had stopped a little while ago, and the second-hand booksellers had warily removed the plastic sheets from the rows of books laid out along the low stone wall of the park. Yashe had no money for books, but obeying the impulse of the lifelong reader, he stopped and turned over several titles. The vendor didn't bother speaking, but looked at him skeptically from under a woollen beanie while stepping from foot to foot on the still-frozen ground.

Yashe found a tattered folio of Chagall reproductions, crudely printed in the old Soviet style. If he'd had a few griven he could spare he would have bought it, just to get lost for a little while in those evocations of the shtetl; the chickens in the street, the cows in the living room, the larger-than life fiddler Chagall had painted, perched on the roof of the house under the swirling stars. And most of all, hovering in the air above the mean, crooked rooftops, the old, bearded man carrying a sack; 'der luft mensch', the floating man, 'gegen iber di heisen', going over the houses; that is, begging from door to door. Looking down at the badly printed reproduction in his hands Yashe felt the old man with the sack to be his ancestor, his grandfather, his great-grandfather, and why not, it might well have been so. Often enough Yashe felt as light and hollow as a floating man himself.

He put the book down. The vendor snorted, as if to say he'd known all along that the likes of Yashe weren't going to buy even a ten-griven book, and Yashe's pretence of looking hadn't fooled him at all, what did you expect from such people?

Yashe left the bookstalls with regret and walked on toward the Privoz market. The chestnut trees that thronged the middle of the park were bare of leaves. A crow sat on a branch reaching above the footpath, and as Yashe walked underneath, it called out, slowly and, it sounded, derisively. *I don't know why you laugh at me, old bird*, thought Yashe, *you are not trusted either, you too are blamed for bad luck.*

Two policemen sauntered down the centre of the paved avenue that ran through the park from south to north. Rather than hurry across in front of them, Yashe paused for them to pass. They did no more than glance at him. A comfortable smell of vodka came from them.

Some coloured rags that looked like women's clothes were spread out to dry on a bush. Yashe knew that at least one old woman lived in this park, no doubt kicked out of her flat by somebody and powerless to do anything about it, having no choice but to sleep here, behind an empty kiosk or in a bus shelter.

Reaching the corner of the block, he went down the steps into the underpass beneath Panteleimonskaya Street. He paid no attention to the people peddling things on the concrete stairs and in the concrete tunnel beneath the street. He walked carefully, as the soggy sheets of cardboard, spread out where the water had pooled, moved treacherously underfoot.

Coming up the steps on the other side he threaded his way through the cluster of small stalls selling shoelaces and brushes and batteries until he reached the footpath outside the Privoz market.

He was not here for any reason except that he needed some money. He had nothing to sell, and nobody owed him money who had the slightest chance of repaying him. Yashe was not a thief, the crowds in the Privoz did not attract him for that reason, but just as on many other days, he had a feeling that to be amongst people gave him a better chance of coming into some money than sitting alone in his single room waiting for something to happen.

He ducked through a gap between two stalls and through a door into the dairy produce hall. The air in there had its own special smell, a combination of sour milk and brine and scrubbed wood. He walked past the big tables piled up with wheels of hard cheese and cubes of white fetta, plastic bottles of kefir and kvass and buckets of sour cream, then past the stalls selling halva and olives and pickled cucumbers, until he came out into the main market square. As always, it was crowded, jostling, and noisy.

He could hear music, not the homogenised thump of recorded music but the vibration of instruments being played in the open air. It seemed to be coming from the far end of the market, and he walked towards the sound.

Over on the eastern side of the Privoz, near the fish stalls, a five-piece brass band was playing. That is, five men in big, shapeless jackets and woollen caps, each carrying an instrument, had assembled in one place, almost conspiratorially, and struck up a tune. It was a Russian Gypsy song, and they were playing it fast, almost desperately fast as if to get through it before being interrupted. The two trumpeters were each playing with one hand, while holding up a CD in a plastic sleeve with the other. The tuba player was, in accordance with tradition, a big, thick-necked, red-faced fellow, standing a head taller than the rest.

They have come in on the bus from Nikolaev or somewhere, and they will get in two or three tunes and sell perhaps two CDs here before the women running the fish stalls start to complain, against which there is no defence, and then they will move on to another part of the market, then another part of the town, and end up trying their luck in Cathedral Square, Yashe thought. But for now they are playing here, a simple pleasure to hear them, a welcome ray of energy on a cold hungry day.

The band finished the first tune with a blare and the saxophonist immediately counted in the next, *raz dva tri chetiri, one two three four,* another fast song, the tuba player puffing out the beat. People mostly walked past without pausing. Everybody had some business to be about here, even if it was just buying vegetables and eggs, and standing still watching something in the Privoz is an invitation for some kind of unwanted attention or another. Some, though, walked past slowly and a few lingered; mostly dark-complexioned men with moustaches, Georgians, or maybe Uzbeks. One man – a foreigner, by his face and overcoat, perhaps even a German – held out twenty griven to one of the trumpeters. With one hand, without missing a note, the musician took the money and handed over a CD.

Beyond the patch of ground where the band was playing was a wall made of sheets of pressed tin. Pushed up against it, looking as if it could be abandoned at any moment if need be, was a second-hand stall, piles of clothes heaped on a trestle table, spilling over onto the ground. A woman Yashe hadn't seen at the Privoz before was in charge of it. She was maybe thirty, with home-dyed blonde hair, a sharp, heavily pockmarked face, and large, liquidly beautiful eyes. She wore a dirty pink tracksuit and house slippers. She leaned with one hip against the table, eating strips of dried fish from a plastic packet.

Yashe was sharply reminded that he was hungry. He was usually able to get more or less enough to eat, although there had been times when he'd had to spend whole days in bed hungry and unable to do anything about it. For the last forty-eight hours, though, he'd had little more than black tea.

He had scarcely any money, but to stop his hunger distracting his sense of opportunity, he bought a round loaf of Georgian bread for four grivni. He tore off a part to eat as he walked around and stuffed the rest in the pocket of his padded coat.

Bypassing the long trestle tables of the fruit and vegetable sellers, he walked briskly toward a green corrugated iron shed with a single small window cut into it, which a man sometimes opened to sell plastic cups of dark raw honey, chunks of honeycomb, and wax candles. In every season but the deepest snow of winter the window had a few bees floating around it. Whenever he saw these bees Yashe wondered why they were there; had they come to try to get their honey back?

Today the window was open, and for another four grivni Yashe bought two brown beeswax candles. The thin, sandy-haired vendor wrapped them in a twist of newspaper. His deft hands looked as if they were made of wax, smooth, yellow, opaque. Yashe tucked the candles carefully into the inside pocket of his heavy coat. A few minutes later, as they warmed, a smell of honey came from them; such a rich smell in the cold air that it was almost as good as having something to eat.

Four grivni would have bought quite a lot, another Georgian loaf or a chunk of sweet, sticky halva or enough buckwheat for a couple of bowls of hot porridge. But the candles were Shabbat candles for that evening, and it was better to have Shabbat candles than food. You could eat, and then tomorrow you needed to eat again, nothing was gained, but to observe Shabbat meant you were in a state of righteousness, and therefore still with a chance of something good happening. At present, that something good would be some money, even a little.

Yashe had nothing he could turn into money, and he had gone hungry before rather than pawn the one valuable thing he owned, his clarinet. It was old, made of real blackwood, good Turkish craftsmanship. A box of reeds had come with the clarinet when he bought it, lovely natural hand-shaved reeds, almost impossible to get these days when the shops have only plastic. He treasured the box of reeds almost as much as the clarinet.

If you owned a musical instrument you could stand on the street corner and play, but nobody would give you anything for playing the clarinet. If you had an accordion, like the old fellow who claimed to have been in Stalingrad as a little boy, and you played patriotic songs, you'd make enough to eat, but not from playing klezmer tunes on a clarinet. Indeed, if the wrong people walked past you when you were playing that kind of music, you might get abused, or even beaten up.

Across the road from the Privoz was a row of condemned houses, the end houses of the row half-demolished, the rest still standing despite boarded up windows and crumbling walls. The doorways were mostly covered with corrugated iron, but one gaped open. A woman stood in its black space, shouting at someone inside. She stepped half-through the doorway and dragged out a black nylon sports bag, which she threw on the footpath. As Yashe watched a pair of feet in boots appeared through the doorway, followed by legs. Then a man emerged, frog-like, on his back, using his arms and legs to propel himself feet-first through the door. It struck Yashe he had seen precisely this pose in a painting by Bosch, a painting of damnation and suffering.

Once on the footpath the man somehow got to his knees and then stood upright. As soon as he was on his feet he set off down the street, walking with a strange mechanical gait, his head immobile. He ignored the sports bag. Yashe could see that blood was oozing from one of the man's eyes, and more seemed to have clotted in his hair, but he walked on like an automaton until Yashe lost him from view.

Walking through the Privoz had not shown Yashe any means by which he might come into money. He headed toward the back of the markets, past the stalls selling smuggled Romanian and Moldavian cigarettes. Just as well I don't smoke, he thought. You can go without food for a while if you have to, but if you smoke, you have to find some tobacco somehow to get through the day, and there was competition if you wanted to pick up the discarded butts around the bus and tram stops.

He slipped though the half-open gate at the back of the market, past the women who had come in from the countryside to sell dried red berries from big plastic bags, past the stinking toilet block, and past the big rubbish bins, stepping carefully over jagged pieces of broken bottles.

Behind the market the cold air stung his face and made his eyes water. He looked around. Men in leather jackets stood about smoking, concentrating as if smoking was an occupation in itself. In front of one of the small hardware shops, standing amongst the wheelbarrows and piles of plumbing pipe, three men were arguing, but listlessly, as if they already knew the outcome. A young guy pushed a flat trolley along the footpath straight at Yashe, so that he had to step back into a doorway to avoid it.

On the other side of the street was the unofficial market, where people gathered each day in the narrow space left between the walls of the old glass factory and the tram tracks to buy and sell whatever they could. Most of the wares were just spread out on the frozen ground; old clothes, worn-out Chinese shoes, used packs of cards, cassette tapes, rusty tools.

One or two of the more regular vendors set up card tables; there they sold old banknotes, parts for Soviet watches, medals from the last war, sometimes pieces of camouflage uniform and fur hats. Yashe liked to visit one of these sellers, a guy named Yuri, from Donetsk. Yuri sold whatever he had found to sell, but specialised in musical instruments. He usually had one or two damaged old domras or balalaikas or accordions, or some pieces of them. The two were on greeting terms, because Yashe had once, after a well-paid gig, bought a Czech *Jolana Star* electric guitar from Yuri for three hundred griven.

Yashe crossed the road and walked along the line of the stalls. At the end of the narrow defile by the tram tracks the ground opened up to a flat, muddy area where trucks parked when the factory was working. Today a Gypsy woman with a full mouth of gold teeth was selling cutlery there; she sat on an upended suitcase with knives and forks and other pieces on a cloth at her feet. A man and woman with the red, blurred features of full-time alcoholics sat nearby on milk crates with a mound of rags, which might have been old clothes, in front of them. The man was telling the woman something in a loud, hoarse voice, gesturing repeatedly with one hand; she sat solidly on her crate, fists on her heavy thighs, occasionally laughing through her toothless mouth.

Yuri was not there today, a shame, not that Yashe could have bought anything from him, but it never hurt to speak to people, you might find out something that helped you, gave you some opportunity. It was getting colder and colder, and Yashe stuck his hands into his armpits, careful not to bend the candles in his pocket.

He felt a touch on his elbow. He looked round cautiously; Leonid was grinning at him. They shook hands. Leonid was a bass guitarist with whom Yashe played when there was work. He could play anything from the *Concerto d'Aranjuez*, solo, to Dixieland. Unusually for a Jew he was heavy drinker, and today he was clearly hung over, his eyes red and puffy, and his hair hanging lankly around his face.

They walked back toward the Privoz together, stepping carefully on the broken ground, moving aside to allow a van that splashed through the greasy mud to pass by. Leonid had a gig that night at the blues club with a guitarist from Kharkov. He might be able to get Yashe in on a job at the Masterskaya cafe next Sunday night, playing old Odessa songs; otherwise things were quiet. They shook hands again and parted on the corner near the bus terminus.

Watching the back of Leonid's maroon leather jacket as he walked away, Yashe felt the moment to find money had passed him by; he couldn't say how exactly but it felt that way to him. He could see nothing else to do but go home; it was already early afternoon and he had to be back by evening anyway, the start of Shabbat. He did not have the fare for a marshrut bus and would have to walk. It was only a dozen blocks, nothing except that it was so cold.

He set off toward Panteleimonskaya Street. Out the front

32

of the market the pavements were full of people. The wind was blowing directly along the street, and there were strips of hardened, smooth ice running along the gutters. The road was clogged with traffic. Marshrut buses were pushing nose to tail to get across the intersection, heedless of the traffic lights and of the car drivers who swore and beeped their horns angrily at them.

Near the corner of the block a number of cars were parked up on the footpath. A fat man leant against the bonnet of a rusty white Volga. The front passenger door was hanging open. Yashe, waiting to cross the street, saw two people laden with bags speak to the driver, each offering a price for a ride. Both times the fat man shook his head briefly; the second time, to emphasise his rejection, he spat into the gutter.

Yashe crossed the road and walked along past the church to Bazarna Street. A knot of people stood at the stop outside Spartak stadium, where the buses that ran into the town centre pulled up. A banner, advertising a football match played three weeks ago, hung above the gates to the stadium, one corner of it untied and flapping in the wind, so that he couldn't make out the visiting team's name. Through the fence he saw crows walking about aimlessly on the soggy green pitch. He edged past the waiting people and set off down the hill.

Bazarna Street was deserted. A woman wearing a bright blue puffer jacket pushed a pram up the hill toward him, but once she had passed, Yashe saw no-one else on the block. The sky was still a dirty milk colour, but it seemed to press down on him even lower than before. The trees that lined the street were bare. The chilly wind got in under the collar of his coat and down his back; he couldn't feel warm, even though he was walking quickly. The cold made his back ache and the pain in his kidneys he woke with each day jabbed into him sharply. He walked under the green cross advertising a chemist's shop, past the ballet school, and then along a grey row of post-war apartment buildings. A heavyset man wearing a flat leather cap appeared on the steps of a shop, carrying four big plastic bottles of beer in his arms. He looked at Yashe briefly, his round red face expressionless, then crossed the road.

By the time Yashe stood in front of the scarred, heavy wooden door that was the entrance to the communal apartment where he lived, his hands were so numb that he dropped his keys getting them out of his pocket. He had to feel for them on the ground in the semi-darkness of the courtyard.

Once inside his room he locked and bolted the door, then plugged in the kettle to make tea. The hot water radiator was working, and the room itself, although the ceiling was high above his head, was not particularly cold. The big window admitted a soft grey afternoon light, enough to see clearly, and he did not turn on the electric bulb.

He carefully laid the two Shabbat candles on the table under the window. With the approach of evening he would light them.

That was an hour or so away, though. Taking off his coat he remembered with pleasure that there was nearly half a round of bread stuffed in the side pocket. He took it out, in its flimsy plastic bag, and put it next to the candles. He would eat it when his tea was brewed, and with that and the radiator, he would warm up quickly. An hour until Shabbat began.

Yashe took down his clarinet in its flannel cloth from the shelf. He carefully unwrapped it and ran his fingers over the German silver keys; they all worked freely.

He could not play on Shabbat, of course; on Shabbat you could make shir, song, but you couldn't make zemer, instrumental music. So he would put the instrument aside at sunset, once Shabbat began, although to Yashe it seemed a pity; the clarinet so closely resembled a human voice that their vibration up in the heavens must be very similar.

He had an hour. He put the mouthpiece to his lips, blew into it once to check the reed, and began to play.

He began with an old klezmer tune, *Konrad's Khoseidl*, and ran through its changes, then improvised simple variations to the tune. His hands began to warm up, and his fingers softened and went more swiftly to where he wanted them until they took over, and went ahead of his thoughts, playing the instrument themselves, developing a melody, changing it, moving into a minor key, then bringing it back to major.

Somehow a part of the Mozart clarinet quintet he had learned at the conservatorium crept into the improvisation, and he gave it full rein. The long hours in the study halls playing the piece came back to him, a trial then but now a pleasure, the diligent practice bringing fruit in music untouched by hesitation. The sweet warm woody notes of the clarinet filled the room. Yashe revelled in the logical, balanced Baroque phrases. They led him back to the original tune, and once there he broke off, unsure what to do with it next.

He felt he was being watched. He looked toward the window. Sitting on the deep sill outside was a big rough-furred orange cat. Yashe knew him, and fed him when he could. I hadn't turned the light on, but the music told him I was home, he thought. 'Sorry, my old orange friend, I don't have anything to eat myself, let alone to give to you,' he called out. The cat sat back on his haunches, wrapped its tail about itself, and watched Yashe, closing and then opening its eyes.

In a sentimental story, Yashe thought, or an educational tale told by a rebbe, somebody, a neighbour with whom I had quarrelled, would have knocked at my door and given me some food, let us say some gefilte fish, as a peace-offering in recognition of the Shabbat. And I would have shared it with the cat, or better yet, given it all to the cat as one of His deserving creatures. That would have been a good start to the Shabbat, a good end to the day, a good end to the tale.

But this is not a sentimental story, Yashe thought, and added out loud, *'And there is no gefilte fish for you or for me, old cat, even though there are plenty of neighbours with whom I have argued.'*

Yashe remembered his tea. It was cold. He looked longingly at the bread, sweating in its thin plastic bag, and felt his stomach pinching, but he once again plugged in the kettle, leaving the bread untouched until the water had boiled and he could make fresh tea. The food and the hot drink together would be far more satisfying than the one without the other. He had tugged off his wet boots on entering the flat, and now stood on the worn floorboards in slippers.

The sky outside was a dark grey. Still a little time before the beginning of Shabbat. Yashe picked up the clarinet again. This time he wanted to play without a melody, without even a predetermined set of chords.

He began hesitatingly with a scale. He played so as to make the notes resonate with the wood of the clarinet, to give them a physical substance, a grounding. He closed his eyes, shutting out the narrow, shabby room, the table littered with rumpled clothes and sheet music and dirty glasses and plates, the low shelf stuffed full of books and papers, the ragged carpet on the floor, and played. He drew on all his skill, all the training he had ever had, every tune he had heard, everything he had ever felt, and played. He played without thought, without plan, without premeditation. He forgot he was hungry, he forgot he had no money and no work, he forgot the pain in his back; he played.

And as he played he saw, inside his closed eyes, patches of bright colour, reds and blues and yellows. They began to solidify into outlines, into things he recognised; a red cockerel, a blue cart, a yellow house; a village street in summer, lined with plum trees. He saw a cow. He saw a kitchen with wooden floorboards, a rough table, bottles and glasses. He saw people sitting, wedding guests, a groom, a veiled bride. He saw the tiled stove, the chimney reaching through the roof, and then a man sitting up on the ridgepole, straddling the roof, playing the violin for the guests. Above that he saw a night sky, spreading wide over the roofs of the houses. And across the sky, above the houses, he saw the floating man, *der luft mensch*, the weightless old man with the sack over his shoulder, moving slowly, horizontally, through the starry sky.

The music Yashe played was music he had never played before, never heard before; it was music arising from the earth but free of the earth. Yashe felt for the first time in his life that the music he played came from his soul. It came out through the clarinet but it was unadulterated by that, the music he played was simply an expression of the desire of the soul to rise up in praise, surrendering its existence to be reunited with its source. He knew without doubt that it was the music spoken of in the prayer: *And the ophanim, and the holy chayot, with a mighty sound, rise toward the seraphim, and facing them, offer praise.*

And Yashe offered praise, he stood before the Throne and offered his soul's praise. He felt as light as a feather, still lighter

36

yet, as light as a speck of dust in a sunray.   And he understood why the beggar with the sack was called *der luft mensch,* the air man, the floater, and he understood why the beggar was said to go 'over' the houses, because he truly did float, he was in the world, but he was above the world.   He was a beggar for the sake of it, because it was his profession, and because his begging was his gift to all those who gave to him and even to those who did not.   He was free and light, unburdened by possessions, by obligations, not weighted down with anything at all.   He was so empty and light that he floated

Yashe too, floated as he played, he floated like his great-grandfather, his ancestor, he floated like the old man with the sack, whom Chagall saw above Vitebsk, but who in truth hovered above every town where his people were.   Yashe played on.   And on. After a time he sensed he was returning to the ground, lightly, slowly, and he realised that the music was drawing itself to a close, his playing had run its course.   He had returned to the scale where he began, and descended down the notes of the scale more and more slowly until he ended with a soft exhalation that barely sounded the reed, a note that was simply a breath, no more than a breath, a slow long breath vibrating very slightly in the air, if it vibrated at all.

Yashe opened his eyes, surprised to find himself simply a man with eyes that opened and closed, a man holding a wooden cylinder banded with German silver in his hands, red clumsy-looking hands emerging from the frayed cuffs of an old sweater.

He realised he was facing the single window of his flat, the window looking out onto the street.   Outside the sky was entirely dark.   The Shabbat had begun. He hastily placed the clarinet on the table and said a prayer asking for forgiveness for violating the Day. And as it was now Shabbat, he could not even dry or wipe clean the wooden clarinet.   He stared at the instrument as it lay on the table for a long minute, then picked it up and cleaned it with the flannel, reciting again the prayer for forgiveness as he did so.

Then he collected the two candles, stood them in two saucers on the windowsill, and lit them with a plastic lighter someone had left in his room after a rehearsal.

In the glow of the candles he saw the orange cat still on

the other side of the glass, sitting upright, its front paws straight up and down, its eyes narrowly slitted. Yashe tugged the window open. It was difficult; the old wood had warped, and he had never been able to get the sash to lift far, even in summer. He opened it as much as he could and stepped back; a blast of freezing air came in. The cat ducked its head once or twice to look into the room and then slowly stepped across the windowsill and down onto the cluttered table. Yashe dragged the window down again with a bang. The cat, once again motionless, sat looking at him.

Ah, old cat, I know you; you too have been all your life going from house to house, from door to door, begging. You know exactly how it is. You have nothing, but you are proud, you might be hungry, but you make no complaint. And because you do not complain you do not suffer, you are free.

Yashe tore off a small piece of his bread and put it in front of the cat. The cat lowered his head carefully to investigate; he twice touched the bread lightly with his nose, then raised his head again and looked at Yashe. Sorry, old friend, said Yashe, that is all I have. At least I tried to share it with you.

The orange cat turned and stepped up to the window again, and Yashe, with some effort, opened stiff wooden frame and let him out. The cat leapt down from the sill onto the pavement. Yashe saw his questioning curved tail vanish in the darkness.

Once the window was closed again and the inrush of cold air had ceased, the candle flames settled back to a steady burning. Yashe pulled his one chair up to the small table and sat down. He ate, deliberately slowly, the remaining portion of the bread, and he sipped his cold tea.

Between now and nightfall tomorrow he could not work, he could not play music, he could not do anything to obtain money, and there was nothing at all to eat. Still, He will provide, thought Yashe. And if not, then it will be my fault, not His.

He finished the tea, and picked up the last crumbs of bread on his fingertip. He was suddenly very tired, and the room was colder than before, despite the radiator. He took down his overcoat from its nail. Holding it in one hand, he climbed up the short ladder to the bed he had constructed on top of his bookshelves, up under the ceiling. He wrapped the overcoat round his shoulders, then drew his two blankets over himself and lay down. Only the glow of the candles below him lit the room. Their light was faint, but pleasant, and it seemed to bear a faint sent of honey. Yashe closed his eyes. Again he saw the starry sky over Vitebsk, over Wilno, over Czernowitz, over Odessa. The stars multiplied and expanded in all directions, thousands, millions of them, and the sky reached up from the earth to the heavens, the houses shrinking down and then disappearing, so all that remained was the black starry sky.

And yet, up there in space, up there in the windless blackness of space, floated the luft mensch, the man with the sack. Yashe saw his face, old, impossibly old, wise and grave and serious and sad, but then the luft mensch started to laugh, a big open-mouthed laugh, and he laughed and laughed, and tears ran down his cheeks into his stubbly beard. And Yashe understood that the luft mensch was Him, was Himself, and that all his life he had been so close to Him he could have touched Him, only he didn't know.

And with that knowledge Yashe dropped off to sleep, and he fell into a deep dreamless sleep, and he knew nothing of what happened around him.

In the streets outside a light snow had begun to fall. First it touched the tops of the houses and apartment buildings and the domes of the churches, and then it reached the pavements and parks and yards, covering them with a dusting of white. And people who were still outside hurried to get indoors, hurried homeward with small flakes of white dancing in the air about them.

Unseen above the buildings, above the streets, hovered an old man, suspended somehow horizontally in the air, with a sack over his shoulder. He floated over the houses and the buildings, and he saw in odd windows below Shabbat candles glowing. But to him all windows were the same, candles or not, and all people were the same, awake, asleep, believing, not believing, drunk, sober, in boisterous company, alone. And he looked down on them all with compassion, the luft mensch; they did not know they existed only because of him, and he did not require it of them that they understood that, or of very few of them anyway. Better for most of them that they slept, like Yashe, that they slept unaware of what had already happened, and what was, and what would happen.

Over all the city the luft mensch spread out his sack, and sleep came to those in the city who needed peace, who needed forgetfulness, who needed respite between now and tomorrow. The luft mensch gathered their sleeping souls in his sack, and in that absolute darkness they slept dreamlessly.

The snow piled up softly in the yard of Yashe's apartment building. It lay in a thick blanket on the windowsills, and along the bare branches of the trees. The sky hung low above, soft and purple. Water dripped from gutters. A big orange cat crept unseen through a gap in a grating and into a basement. The Shabbat candles in Yashe's window guttered, one after the other, and went out. The room fell into darkness. Yashe slept on. He knew nothing at all of tomorrow, he did not suffer for thinking of tomorrow; he slept, he was at peace.

***

Summer Skin
Richard Larson

Richard Larson was born in West Africa, has studied in Rhode Island and worked in Spain, and at 23 now writes from Edmonton, Alberta. He was a semifinalist for the Norman Mailer Poetry Prize and his short work has been nominated for the Pushcart Prize and Journey Prize. He appears in magazines such as Word Riot, decomP, Bartleby Snopes, Monkeybicycle, Prick of the Spindle, and many others. Find him at richwlarson.tumblr.com.

Summer Skin, Richard's rather Chekhovesque entry to the Aestas 2015 enthralled the judges. As Judge Leela Panikar puts it "a very smooth narrative where the details are very well woven. The strong dialogues carry the story along, the characters are realistically portrayed, their motivations easily understood".

Elliot is sitting on the sofa when Corbin comes out of the bathroom hallway with a ratty brown towel around his hips and Elliot's book clutched in his wet hand. He laughs high and sharp, waving it side to side so the alien eyes on its cheap holographic cover flash. Elliot hauls up off the imploding cushions and snatches it away.

His cousin grins. "So that's what you do in the field all day," he says, shaking his head. "You're actually, seriously looking for crop circles. Jesus."

Heat leaks into Elliot's cheeks. He doesn't say that sightings and even abductions are shockingly common out in rural areas. He doesn't say that he would rather be anywhere than inside his aunt's trailer with its peeling floral wallpaper and the stink of the unspayed cat that slinks in and out at will and, of course, Corbin.

"It's just a book," Elliot says, pretending to watch the talk-show drone on the television. "Just something to read."

"Your mom didn't give you it, did she?" Corbin asks. "She didn't slip you it last visit?"

"Ten-cent bin," Elliot mutters, still not looking up.

"What'd you say?" Corbin wraps his wiry arm around Elliot's neck from behind; Elliot squirms away from the knuckles kneading his scalp. "What'd you just say, Elliot?"

"I said fuck off, I found it in a ten-cent bin." Elliot tries to keep his voice even. He can feel his heart thrumming up his throat. A familiar shock of sweat under his arms, at his groin. Then Corbin's arm vanishes. Elliot's panic slowly subsides.

"And you don't believe it, do you?" his cousin asks, slouching onto the couch beside him. He is only two years older but takes up twice the space, knees jacked apart, arm sprawled across the back. He picks a silvery strand of cat hair off the fabric.

"Believe what." Elliot clutches the book hard between his

hands.

"Aliens." Corbin waggles his tongue, bugs his eyes. "You don't believe that shit, right?"

Elliot doesn't say that his mother showed him the implant the aliens imbedded under her blotched red skin. He doesn't say that sometimes in the night he can hear the eerie hum of their transmissions, and his mother heard it too, louder and louder in the days before they made her check herself in.

"Or are you craaazy like her?" Corbin asks, soft and sing-song.

"It's just a book," Elliot repeats.

"Good," Corbin says. "Had me worried, there, Ellie." He heaves himself off the sofa, hiking the towel back up around his hips, and Elliot lets himself breathe easy. He stares at the flickering television. Safe again, and his aunt will be back in a few hours.

Corbin returns without warning, slides his arms up under Elliot's armpits and locks his fingers over the back of his neck, forcing his head down. Elliot freezes. His cousin flops on top of him, dead weight. Elliot gives an experimental twist. Nothing. He feels Corbin's scratchy chin against his shoulder blade. The panic comes back.

"Wrestle me," Corbin says. A drop of water from his wet hair splatters onto the nape of Elliot's neck.

–

The next day, Elliot goes out to the fields again. He takes his splitting backpack, the one he packed a week's worth of clothes into nearly a month ago. Now it holds his book, a rumpled Dasani one-litre, and a pair of bruising bananas Elliot takes from the kitchen counter. He leaves when his aunt is leaving for work, letting himself out the door while she stirs St. Patrick's from the liquor cabinet into her instant coffee. She suggests he pry Corbin's lazy ass away from the Playstation later on and get him to go exploring, too.

Elliot nods to her from safe behind the screen door. He

44

doesn't plan to come back until his iPod is dead and his stomach is gnawing itself to pieces.

Outside, the canola fields are bright poisonous yellow against the clear blue sky. Their pungent smell slides into his nostrils and settles in the back of his throat like oil. Elliot walks in wide circles. First he listens to Summer Skin on repeat, then switches to the Feint megamix that can last him for hours. Sometimes he has to clamber over a sagging wire fence, when he goes from canola to hayfield, and sometimes he runs away from the drone of a combine with a sunburned farmer perched on top.

But for the most part, he's uninterrupted. He walks slowly, relishing the scrape of stalks against his trackies, the hot clean pulse of the sun on his cheeks and bare neck. He knows from the book that the aliens make their crop circles as a way to mark out important areas, potential abduction sites. He hasn't found any yet.

His mother was abducted for the first time on her fourteenth birthday. She told him the story in a motel room foggy with cigarette smoke, raking her artery-red nails through his hair, speaking soft and slow and deliberate, nothing like the crazy people Elliot had seen hauling their sleeping bags through Grandin Station or panhandling along Jasper.

She said the aliens didn't have bodies the way humans did, so they had to make props. Stand-ins. Small thin men made of rubbery gray flesh, with flat black eyes that were really only pigment, only painted-on, and mouths that were surgical gashes leading nowhere. She said they were fucking terrifying, but once you were inside the ship itself, swimming through its silvery veins, everything was bright and white and beautiful. That was when they gave her the implant.

She showed him, then, the small black mark on her knobby wrist, and made him hold the bone of it until he could feel the heat and the vibration coming through. Leaning in close to him, smelling like smoke and chemicals, she told him that the aliens were keeping an eye on her. Looking out for her. She was special, and Elliot had the same genetic material, and more likely than not, he was special, too.

Elliot is nearly fourteen. He knows it will happen soon, or

never.

Elliot stops. There are scorch marks on the ground, a sooty black ring where the stalks have been burned down brittle. He crouches, making one of his earbuds tug inside his ear. Between his thumb and fingertip, the end of the stalk turns to charcoal powder. Maybe it's nothing. Maybe it's something, the afterburn from an alien engine.

Taking both earbuds out, Elliot sits and listens. The crops ripple in the breeze like a curtain, susurrating against each other. He can hear insect legs and the distant groan of a truck on the highway. He can hear his own thin breathing. And there, in the back half of his skull, he can hear the faint, high-pitched hum.

-

That evening, Elliot's aunt heats up a can of spaghetti Bolognese and tells him that Corbin is staying over at a friend's for the night, not that he had the decency to let her know ahead of time. Elliot eats until his stomach hurts, partly because he's hungry and partly so he won't have to reply while his aunt gives him the small speech he saw her scribbling onto a piece of loose-leaf, about how his mom is a good person whose mind is in a bad place. Elliot knows better than to listen. His mom told him exactly what everyone would start saying.

She asks him a few questions about how he feels, then gives up and shows him old pictures in an album of her and his mom. In one they are little kids holding hands. Their hair is sun-bleached and their grins are stained with Orangesicle. Their tanned hands, too, freckled fingers gummy with syrup. Summer skin, Elliot thinks. The back of the photo says June '91.

A little while later, Elliot brushes his teeth and goes to bed, sliding the desk chair under the door knob before he climbs onto his double-foamy. The sky is dark outside his window. He tries to sleep, but can't. He hears the wind picking up to a howl, the apple trees bent over at the waist. Bathroom water chokes and snarls through drains. He hears his aunt's feet scratching carpet, her body moving upstairs. A pipe clanking. TV on and then off.

He hears his wet pulse in his ears, and below it all, growing louder and louder, he hears the hum. It bounces around in his skull until he can't stand it anymore. He swings himself out of bed with his legs slicked in goose-bumps. As quietly as he can, he moves the chair away from the door and sneaks out, not bothering to change out of his baggy pajama pants.

In the kitchen, he slips one of the black-and-yellow solar flashlights from the drawer. In the dark entryway, he pulls his jacket on over his bare chest, where he can feel his heart hammering his ribs. The fabric is cold on his hot skin. He forces his way into one worn Skecher and then the other.

Elliot guides the screen door shut behind him, praying the rusted spring won't squeak. It doesn't. He slips off the porch and is heading down the gravel drive when two headlights suddenly round the far bend. Elliot stumbles down into the ditch and kneels there, still. The sputtering battered Nissan crawls forward. Elliot recognises it as Nat's, Nat who sometimes makes Corbin give Elliot a go on NBA2K when she's over. The car slides to a halt just a few meters off him. He can hear Corbin's high sharp laugh from inside, and in the orange light of Nat's blunt he can see them fighting over the satellite radio.

Nat leans over him to open the door. "Letting you out here, alright?"

"Fuck your dad, man," Corbin says.

Nat says something about not baby-sitting him again, about her dad being pissed when he finds out about the liquor. Corbin calls her a cunt; Nat shoves him out of the passenger side. He hammers on the door a few times, but she's locked it from the inside. He pushes his tongue against the window like a pink slug. She flips him off, waves, and reverses back down the drive. The Nissan's engine gurgles. Corbin sways in her beams, light taking the colour out of his face and blacking both eyes. He doesn't have an expression. He turns and slouches his way toward the house.

Elliot heads for the field.

-

The night air is cold flint in his lungs and the sky overhead is all stars. Elliot goes on autopilot, retracing his route through the field, slithering through the stalks. He's in such a hurry he sticks his thumb on a ragged wire hopping the low fence. The flashlight strobes the air in front of him, and he can hear the hum so loud it throbs his jaw. Everywhere he looks, he sees the gray men peering at him through the curtain of crops. His chest is tight with terror and joy.

When he gets to the burn mark, he sits down, cross-legged, with his flashlight pointing up from his lap into the sky. It's vast and dark out here, nothing like the streetlamp-smothered night he watched from the apartment window in Edmonton. The stars are huge, almost close enough to touch. Any moment now, one will detach itself from the blackness, swell and descend.

"Take me, take me, take me," Elliot mutters, moving the flashlight in a slow circle. "Come on. Please." He can hear his heartbeat in his ears, and feel it in his cut thumb. He breathes deep, trying to concentrate on the hum. It's getting quieter, or maybe higher. The cold air crackles with it.

He'll swim through the ship's weightless corridors. They'll put the implant in his wrist and tell him he matters. They'll keep him safe, and later, when his mother is out of the hospital, he'll show her the black mark on his sunned skin, and she'll be so happy she'll cry.

A bright white light flashes into Elliot's eyes. Something steps out of the crop, a stretched silhouette. Elliot's heart hammers into his throat.

"What the fuck are you doing out here?" Corbin demands. He flashes him with the light again, the second flashlight from the kitchen drawer. Elliot's veins freeze over. He wishes that he'd taken both.

He says nothing.

"I know you're not sleepwalking," Corbin says, turning off the flashlight. His voice has a liquor slur to it. "Take me, take me. You're waiting around for a UFO to come down and pick you up. Do you even realise how fucking crazy that is?"

Elliot's mouth is bone dry. He casts another quick glance

48

up to the sky.

"You're hoping they pick you up and do all those tests on you, right?" Corbin grins. "That's what you're hoping for. A good probing. Right?" His teeth are still bared, but now it's not a grin. "Turn off your light."

Corbin is only two years older, but so much faster, so much heavier, and it only takes a moment before Elliot is pressed hard to the ground. He hears his cousin pick up his dropped flashlight and click it off. He can't hear the hum anymore, just his own panicked breathing and the sliding of fabric. He wants to howl like he did the first time, but his throat is full of ice.

Elliot quietly begs for the ship to come down, for the gravity to freeze them in place and then gently pull him inside, with his hair standing on end and his clothes floating around him, lifting him up and away from Corbin.

But when his aunt showed him the old picture, she pointed to his mom's wrist, where the black birth mark had always been.

And when he sees Corbin's face in his peripheral, his cousin's eyes are only pigment, painted-on, leading nowhere.

***

How Do You Know
Fred McGavran

Fred McGavran is a graduate of Kenyon College and Harvard Law School, and served as an officer in the U.S. Navy. After retiring from the practice of law, he was ordained a deacon in the Episcopal Church. Fred is a multiple award recipient including an Individual Achievement Award from the Ohio Arts Council for *The Reincarnation of Horlach Spencer*, a story that appeared in *Harvard Review*, and the Raymond Carver award for his collection of short stories *The Butterfly Collector* (published by Black Lawrence Press) Won. More information on Fred is available at www.fredmcgavran.com.

Impressed by *How Do You Know*, Judge Brett Alan Sanders says "A wholly original story, exploring with seemingly effortless humor and a light Borgesian wit, questions of knowledge and, from a myriad of angles, the problem of death. Nothing like it under the sun."

On a rare weekend off, Lewis Maudlin, M.D. began to wonder if he had died. He was paging through the second section of the paper when he saw a familiar name in the obituaries. Now who can this be, he wondered. He didn't recognise the decedent's picture. Aside from the other doctors and administrators at his hospital, he didn't know anyone who could have died. It finally dawned on him that this was a former patient. Now that posed a problem—obviously this person did not die under his care; what made him think he could do it after he was discharged? What good were all his skills, if they died anyway? Why did he bother? If he were dead now, too, how would he know?

He felt his pulse: 76 a minute, and there were three new texts from the hospital asking for orders. How could he be dead if everything was going exactly as before? He had always viewed death as something that happened to other people. In all the journals he had read and all the conferences he had attended, no one had ever addressed how to determine death from the inside. How do you know when you are dead?

After 30 years as an orthopedic surgeon, Dr. Maudlin had seen and treated every injury the human skeleton could suffer, from broken heads to fractured toes. Endless stories of accidents and assaults followed by examinations, x-rays, operating rooms, surgical instruments and blood blended into a routine of listen, touch, see and cut. Days or weeks later, he removed the bandages and casts, and sent the patient off to endure all the other vagaries of human life.

The routine was so engrossing, and the thanks of patients, the admiration of colleagues, and the money so rewarding that he did not miss his three former wives or the children they had taken with them. Sex was something he could find from a passing socialite at a fund raiser, and love was not part of his routine. How could death, even his own, interrupt a process as self-contained as a perpetual motion machine?

All morning Dr. Maudlin grappled with the problem. He

replied to the texts, and more came; the operating room for his Monday morning surgery was changed; everything seemed normal and the question began to fade until he watched a football game. Two expensively dressed men in headsets shouted statistics and snapped at each other faster than residents on rounds, while two lines of men ran at each other across a field until they collided in spectacular crashes and cartwheels in the air.

Every few minutes, beer companies interrupted the game with vignettes to prove their brand was essential to happiness. The expensively dressed men argued about which ad was the best, just as they argued about every play. Slowly the feeling that events were meaningless returned; he had watched the same game and the same ads a thousand times before. Nothing would change if one team or the other won; nothing would change if all the beer taps went dry; nothing would change if a whirlwind descended and swept the stadium and all the screaming fans into the air.

That evening the doctor went to a neighborhood Thai restaurant for carry out. He ordered Penang curry at a hotness of 3 and brown rice, just as he always did. Leaving the restaurant, he thought he saw the face of the patient from the obituary page reflected on the door. When he turned around, however, the face had changed into someone else. At first Dr. Maudlin was disturbed by this apparent hallucination, but then he relaxed. No rational person could discern whether he himself had died, from a dead person who had returned to share the experience in a Thai restaurant.

He ate his curry from a tray table in front of the TV, alternately swallowing a mouthful and clicking through the channels. The news was a frightened series of cataclysms and plagues in foreign places and ignorance and corruption at home, unmitigated by any understanding or learning. How many times had he seen the same accidents and murders, the same car bombs, the same naked children crawling in the dust? How many times had he held his breath watching through a bomb sight as a missile descended upon a doomed vehicle below? Despite the slow burning in his stomach, Dr. Maudlin did not feel he was part of it anymore.

There has to be a scientific way to determine whether I am

alive or dead, he thought, as he washed his hands before his first surgery on Monday morning. No physician can rely upon subjective symptoms for such an important event. He had nearly convinced himself that existential angst did not support the radical hypothesis of death, when he found himself watching the operation from overhead, as if he were standing on the ceiling looking down.

After so many years opening up hips and implanting plastic joints, it was time to let one of the younger people do it.

The sense of detachment returned as the team washed up and cleared the operating room. As usual he didn't speak to anyone, and no one met his eyes. What was the use of operating, if the octogenarian patient were only at a way station to a column inch under an old photo on the obituary page? By the time he changed back into his suit, he had decided to consult the chief pathologist. If anyone at the hospital understood the death experience, it was Douglas H. Blinder, M.D.

Dr. Blinder and Dr. Maudlin had been in an unofficial contest for the best dressed department head for a decade. The pathologist preferred a mixture of LL Bean and Banana Republic to emphasize the working aspect of an autopsy; Dr. Maudlin preferred the bow tie accented Brooks Brothers look to emphasize his sophistication and to be prepared for unexpected consults with his financial advisors. Blinder was enjoying a coffee in the snack room after supervising the dissection of the usual Monday morning harvest of corpses from murders and car wrecks in the city and overdoses and suicides in the suburbs.

"Oh, hello, Lewis," the pathologist greeted him. "I wasn't expecting you."

"There's something I want to ask you," Maudlin began.

"Didn't I see something about you in the paper today?"

"Probably something about the sports medicine gala this weekend."

Dr. Blinder did not seem satisfied. Nevertheless, he made the obligatory offer of the last cup of coffee in the pot to his colleague. Dr. Maudlin accepted, suppressing a shudder when

Blinder poured it into a porcelain cup that apparently was cleaned by swiping it with a filthy rag hanging from the faucet.

"Tell me, Douglas, how close you are to the death experience?" Dr. Maudlin inquired to begin the strangest conversation of Dr. Blinder's life.

"They are usually pretty dead when they get to me," the pathologist replied, suspicious that his colleague's visit had some ulterior purpose. "By the way, Lewis, should we move this into my office?"

A striking blond resident, old enough to discern the on the make attire of the successful surgeon but young enough not to appear to be attracted, had entered and was starting a fresh pot of coffee. As they left the room, Dr. Maudlin saw her take a cup from the sink and wipe it out with the dirty rag.

"Well, now," the pathologist began, when they were both seated in the soft light of his exquisitely decorated office. The hospital's requirement that department heads decorate their own offices had induced him to hire a society decorator to make a statement. Maudlin, however, was as oblivious to the statement as the pathologist himself. "Is there something going on in surgery that I should know about?"

"I'm investigating the death experience," Maudlin replied. "Not that I see much of it. But there is a lacuna in the literature that I thought you might be able to fill."

If a resident had talked like that, Blinder would have kicked him out of his office. With Dr. Maudlin, however, he had to be more subtle.

"What's missing, Lewis?"

"Death from the patient's perspective. How do they know they're dead?"

"By definition death is the cessation of all vital functions of the body, including heartbeat, brain activity, and breathing. You lose those, and you don't experience anything."

"As a scientist, I have learned to question every assumed fact," Maudlin said.

Dr. Blinder knew better than to argue with his colleague. On a number of celebrated occasions, the surgeon had invented instruments and developed procedures to overcome problems everyone else thought unsolvable. So, like the good physician that he was, he decided to refer Maudlin to another specialist.

"That's an interesting view of the problem," he said. "Why don't you take it up with Stan Gray in neurology? They're more cutting edge on this sort of thing that we are."

A secretary entered without knocking, carrying hard copies of the morning's autopsies for the pathologist's signature. Something on the first page made them both look at Maudlin with renewed curiosity.

"Thanks, Douglas," Dr. Maudlin said. "I'll do that."

For a second Dr. Blinder considered giving Dr. Gray a warning call but decided not to. It would be more fun to compare notes if the neurologist approached it cold.

Dr. Maudlin caught Dr. Gray as he was returning to his office after a morning lecture at the medical school. The hospital's youngest department head wore sneakers, designer jeans and a black T-shirt that made his name badge and title stand out.

"Everybody's talking about you, Lewis," he said, appearing surprised to see him.

"I hope it's something good," Maudlin joked.

The neurologist did not immediately reply.

"Got something for me?" he finally said, as if a little afraid of what the answer might be.

Referrals are the soul of hospital politics.

"I have a question, Stanley," Maudlin replied, following Gray into his office, where a glass wall of degrees and honors faced the visitor from behind the neurologist's desk. "How does a patient know when he's dead?"

It took Dr. Gray a second to recover from the sexist language.

"Death is an absence of all perception," he replied. "There is nothing to feel, nothing to report."

"I heard the same thing in pathology," Maudlin replied.

Dr. Gray was stunned. An unfavourable comparison of his specialty with pathology by the chief of surgery could threaten his year-end bonus.

"Of course there are near death experiences," he said to regain the momentum. "The patient has the sensation of floating over the operating table into a gold or a black tunnel, where angels or demons lie in wait."

Maudlin recalled his experience floating over his operating table, but he had not encountered any angels or demons.

"And then returns to tell about it," he said. "But the reports are all from people who haven't really died. They just think that they did."

"Is that a problem?"

"This may be some random neurological event, like getting a static shock touching a flashlight with burned out batteries. Besides, how many patients who are close to death and then survive experience this?"

"Very few," Gray admitted.

"Certainly not enough for a valid statistical sample."

"Then of course there are instances of phantom limb," the neurologist countered. "Certainly you must have had cases where the patient loses a limb but continues to feel as if it were still there."

"So death may be the ultimate phantom limb experience," Dr. Maudlin said, intrigued. "The body is dead, but the perception of it continues."

"Yes."

"There could be millions of people walking around who don't know that they're dead," he reflected. "And millions of people who see them and can't figure out what's going on."

As a professional courtesy, the neurologist decided not to reply to Dr. Maudlin's last statement. He was beginning to feel as if he were locked in a room while fire alarm bells were ringing in the corridor.

"Sooner or later, however, the patient stops feeling the phantom limb," he said, hoping to bring the conversation to an end.

"What is doing the perceiving, Stanley?"

Dr. Gray was stumped.

"Are you suggesting that consciousness is not dependent upon the mind?"

"I leave the point open, Doctor."

When one physician calls another "doctor," it is a sign that the conversation has ended. The neurologist had not felt so much relief since he had outmaneuvered three more senior colleagues to become department head.

"You might want to mention this to Melanie Watkins in psychiatry, Lewis," Dr. Gray said, hoping for credit for a referral. "I'm sure she must have some interesting thoughts on the subject."

Maudlin did not catch the irony.

"I'll drop by after my afternoon surgery."

Dr. Gray left a message for Dr. Watkins as soon as the surgeon left his office.

In the elevator to psychiatry after witnessing his second hip replacement of the day, Dr. Maudlin wondered if he had dictated his post op note from what he had actually seen and done or from memory. What if someone compared all his post op hip replacement notes from the past 20 years and discovered they were identical? Did that mean that all the patients were the same, and he was repeating the same ritual day after day, like a penitent assigned the same prayers? But one of the patients was different: one of them had died. It would be comforting if Dr. Watkins had experienced a similar problem.

He found the psychiatrist emerging from the activities room with her knitting, where she had been showing recalcitrant patients the secrets of cross stitching. A large, past middle age woman who wore colourful shawls regardless of the season, she had that tired, weak, searching-for-understanding look that meant so much to patients' relatives and search committees. After the clamor accompanying her appointment as the hospital's first female department head subsided, however, she skillfully guided the department back into its traditional obscurity, like a balloonist descending on a field shielded from the road by trees.

Dr. Watkins led Dr. Maudlin to a consulting room off the activities room. As she closed the door, Maudlin realised she was wheezing.

"How nice to see you, Lewis," she panted. "Would you like a cup of herb tea?"

The psychiatrist was so devoted to empathy that she rarely had time for hospital gossip, voice mails or emails from the hospital administration.

"No, thank you," the surgeon said, stopping himself just before he said "dear." "I've come to ask your advice."

Dr. Watkins did not reply. Taking up her knitting, she was concentrating on a knot she had mistakenly tied in her excitement. "I've come to ask your advice" was the physician's traditional lead-in to an admission of a serious emotional problem.

"I am seeking an insider's view of death," he said, striking at the lure of the silent therapist. "How does a person know whether or not he's dead?"

"Well, Lewis, we know it when we see it, but as for the patient herself, I have never considered the question."

She set down her knitting and fixed him with a ghastly smile that suggested they were approaching a mystic experience together.

"Why are we talking about this?"

Maudlin broke her stare a second before he succumbed.

"The question has enormous clinical implications," he said.

"If I knew I was dead, I would make major changes in my lifestyle."

Now it was the psychiatrist who could not extricate herself from the cobra's stare.

"Tell me more about your dead patients," he said, using the classical therapist's response to a revelation by the patient.

"Oh my, this is getting grisly. Sometimes they leave notes, but I don't think that is what you're looking for."

"No. I want their appreciation of the situation after they're dead, not before."

Dr. Watson spread her hands.

"I have a ward full of people who would love to tell you why they want to die, but no one to tell you what it is like afterwards."

"The absence of complaints may be evidence that they made the right decision," Maudlin said. "That's how we would look at it if we were in retailing. We may not exclude it as a rationale for silence."

Even after thirty-five years in psychiatry, Dr. Watson was having trouble following the conversation. She responded with a nod and a sympathetic smile, which sometimes moved female patients to reveal their wildest fantasies in hopes of prolonging the moment of empathy.

"Thank you, Melanie. This has been very helpful," Maudlin said, standing up.

"It has?"

"To make the correct diagnosis, we must rule out all other possibilities."

That seemed to satisfy Dr. Watkins, but she spent a bad night trying to decide whether to report her colleague to the head of the hospital as a suicide risk. Meanwhile, Dr. Maudlin was taking the stairs back to his office, when he passed a pudgy, balding man in his thirties, wearing a short sleeved dress shirt, Penny's tie, and a badge that said Chaplain. Pursuant to the egalitarian code for staff beneath the rank of physician, only his first name was given.

"Drop by when you have a moment, Jim," Dr. Maudlin called back before they were a few steps apart.

The effect was comparable to the disembodied voice that spoke to the Apostle Paul on the road to Damascus. Jim froze, turned and looked upwards, nearly fell, and reversed direction as fast as he could without twisting an ankle. When they reached the orthopedic floor, Maudlin led the startled chaplain into an office that had been more inaccessible to him than the Holy of Holies in the Great Temple in Jerusalem.

"Jim, you may be the only one here who knows the answer to this," Maudlin began.

The chaplain sat speechless, like a priest at Delphi waiting to receive a petition for an oracle.

"You have been at many bedsides when patients have died."

Jim nodded.

"How does a person know when he is dead?"

"It's difficult to say," he said, afraid that his great moment would pass without satisfying the petitioner. "They stop talking."

Dr. Maudlin was not satisfied.

"What does the Bible say?" he asked, referring to a book he had not spoken of or read since confirmation at the age of thirteen.

"We'll know for sure at the Resurrection of the Dead and the Last Judgment, but as for just being dead, I'm afraid it's silent."

"There might be a hiatus where there is still room for doubt?"

Jim saw a space opening up to escape and took it.

"Before the Resurrection, we are asleep," Jim said a little more confidently.

"'But in that sleep of death what dreams may come . . . .'" Lewis recited from some long ago high school class.

The chaplain glanced at his cell to signal he wanted to disengage.

"Would you like a cup of coffee? Soft drink?" Maudlin offered, wanting to prolong the session.

"I was on my way to a patient in intensive care."

"Oh. Alright. Thanks."

After several hours overseeing residents with follow-up patients and reviewing the charts of his department's surgeries that day, auditing a staff meeting, and dropping in at the retirement party of a long-time surgical nurse, Lewis Maudlin went home, unsatisfied. The rest of the week, like every other week, was filled with operations and patients and meetings, but nothing he had not seen so many times before that he could not be sure it was actually happening or a memory. Despite regular eating, drinking, bathing and normal bodily functions, he felt more and more estranged from a repetitious world.

To make things worse, he had the whole weekend off. If he could make it until 6 o'clock Saturday, however, he could go to the hospital's annual sports medicine gala and mingle happily with people who had not so much as swung a golf club in 30 years.

The sense of alienation intensified as Dr. Maudlin approached the bar, where he exchanged his complimentary drink ticket for a third of a glass of house chardonnay. Then a tour of an hors d'oeuvres table laden with chunks of cheese and crackers, tiny sausages wrapped in dough, supermarket vegetables with ranch dressing, and plates so small it was impossible to carry more than one item away at a time. Exasperated, he let himself go and floated to the ceiling, hoping to avoid detection beside a dazzling chandelier.

I wonder what they're serving for dinner, Maudlin thought, taking another sip.

He was wondering how soon to descend to refill his glass when he noticed a shadow on the other side of the chandelier. Pushing off from the ceiling, he drifted around to it and discovered the blond pathology resident balancing a plate of pigs-in-a-poke in one hand and a glass of red wine in another. She was trying to decide how to eat a sausage without spilling the rest onto the crowd below.

"May I help?" he said, offering to take her plate.

She had taken off her shoes and hung them over two of the electric candles.

"Dr. Maudlin!" she exclaimed. "I didn't expect to see you here."

"After all, it is my department," he replied.

Her name badge said that she was Christie Delight, M.D.

"I never know what to say to people at these things," she said between bites.

"After you've been around awhile, all you have to do is smile, nod, and act like you're heading toward the bar, and you don't have to say anything."

Christie appeared intrigued by this confession. Although Dr. Maudlin usually stayed away from female residents, he was beginning to sense that the sterile atmosphere of her department and staring at stains of dead cells under the microscope were not satisfying all her needs.

"It's even worse when you have to give a ten minute speech welcoming people you've never heard of," he continued, deducing correctly that sharing a problem might be a precursor to intimacy.

"I feel like I'm high," Christie said, taking the paper plate so he could have the last little sausage.

Maybe it was the heat from the lights, maybe it was the wine, but Lewis Maudlin felt more and more drawn to the pathologist.

"All this week I've been having out of the body

experiences and thinking I might have died," he said, surprising himself with a confession he had not intended to make unless necessary to get her the last few yards from his living room to his bed.

Bells were ringing in the hall below, while an anxious maitre d' waved his arms to herd the diners into the banquet room.

"Can we talk later?" he said, feeling himself starting to descend.

"I'd like that," Christie said, waiting to follow until her shoes had cooled enough to put back on.

"I don't think you're dead," the pathologist said as they lay side by side on the huge bed in his master suite.

"What did you think when it first happened to you?" he said, still gripping her hand.

"Sex?"

"No. What we're feeling tonight."

"That I'd been studying too hard."

"But you agree that this is a serious question."

She let go of his hand and turned on her side to face him.

"Why don't you talk to Professor Von Stamn at City University? He has a crazy way of thinking, too."

"What department is he in?"

"Physics. He supervised my senior thesis."

"Physics doesn't deal with death."

"No one in the life sciences has been able to deal with it, Lewis. I'll send you his contact information. Now let's try our own test again.

She touched him in a place that precluded objection, and for a few hours Dr. Maudlin forgot his angst.

"Death is a singularity," Professor Borg Von Stamn said,

swiveling around in his chair to a small blackboard he kept for inspiration. "Like a black hole."

He preferred not to look at people when he was talking, especially medical school faculty. Although they both held the same rank as professor, Dr. Maudlin's compensation was five times that of the physicist.

He sketched something like a cone coffee filter and stopped.

"Do you know calculus?"

Dr. Maudlin nodded. He had not studied calculus in thirty-five years, but he did not want to appear too trusting. Von Stamn was short, unshaven, had not seen a barber in months, and was dressed in jeans and a gray sweatshirt. How could a man like this ever inspire Christie, he wondered.

And then the physicist began to write. The chalk shrieked and spewed dust, equations bubbled across the board, and the little man exploded with an energy that the cold formulae could never contain.

"There!" he exclaimed. "You see it now, don't you?"

Dr. Maudlin nearly did. Like trying to read a French newspaper years after the last exam, enough calculus came back to get the sense.

"Death, like a black hole, is a singularity, a point from which no information can emerge," Von Stamn continued, waving the chalk at the equations covering the cone. "Once a particle enters, even a particle of light, the gravity is so strong that it cannot escape."

"Like the traditional view of death," Maudlin said. "Everything sucked into the black hole is wrapped up so tightly that we can never know what happened to it."

"Unless two of my colleagues are correct," the physicist said, wiping away the cone and the equations with his hand and starting to write again. "Black holes cannot be infinite, or they would absorb all the matter in the universe, and we wouldn't be here. So when the black hole becomes so dense that it cannot be compressed any further, it explodes in a white hole, spewing everything back into space."

Something like a cherry bomb had replaced the cone filter.

"Like the Resurrection of the Dead," Maudlin said.

"In physics we do not think of it that way," Professor Von Stamn said, feeling self-confident enough to turn and look at his guest.

"Neither do we in medicine."

"It looks like you'll have to try philosophy," Christie said that evening over crab Rangoon appetizers in the Thai restaurant.

Dr. Maudlin was frustrated; it was taking longer and longer to get the server's attention. Not sure he was up to another night with her so soon, and still not confident enough in their relationship to confess his liberal use of Viagra, Dr. Maudlin had taken her to dinner after a longer than usual day. Penang curry, he hoped, would live up to its reputation as a natural restorative.

"Did you study philosophy?" he asked, surprised that she had not confined herself to the usual premed regimen of science, mathematics and borderline despair.

"Professor Baklanov persuaded me to transfer from linguistics to pre-med," she said.

"Why?"

"I was taking her course on the philosophy of language, and she said I wasn't the type of person who could spend her life not knowing whether anything she said had any meaning."

After dinner, Lewis Maudlin was relieved when she said she was tired and wanted to go home.

Olga Mikhailovna Baklanov was waiting for Dr. Maudlin beside the samovar in her office. Steaming and shuddering as if about to explode, this cauldron often compelled visitors to enter into a Platonic dialogue with the professor about whether it was safe to remain. Those not convinced by her logic left early, which Olga Mikhailovna interpreted as a sign they would not have understood her conversation anyway. Lewis Maudlin accepted the tea without comment and sat down in a large chair covered by what appeared to be worn out cloth placemats.

"Dr. Delight tells me you are studying the problem of death," the Professor began, maneuvering into a wooden swivel chair behind her desk, where she enjoyed access to stacks of periodicals on her credenza. "Philosophically, it is quite difficult; practically, it cannot be so hard, considering all the people who are able to experience it."

"I am studying death from the inside, from the perspective of the person who dies. How do they know that they're dead?"

"This is something I have never considered before," the philosopher reflected. "Death is a phenomenon that our system of thought cannot comprehend, like Socrates' paradox." "Socrates' paradox?" Maudlin repeated, feeling he was caught up in one himself.

"Socrates' supposed paradox," she replied. "'This statement is not true.'"

"The statement is nonsensical," he said, regaining his self confidence.

"No, Lewis, and neither is your question. Every system of thought, every way of measuring experience, has some phenomena that cannot be comprehended by that system. So Socrates' paradox is not nonsensical; it is a flaw in the system. We often don't know what these flaws are until we stumble over them, as you and I just did, and then we usually ignore them or overwhelm them with a convenient ideology to deny their existence."

"But if the experience of death is an event that cannot be comprehended by our system of thought, what is the answer to my question?"

"We may come upon it while preparing our paper. Although you raised the question, you do agree with me that I should be the first author, don't you?"

Lewis Maudlin left the department of philosophy as

confused as when he entered.

"Where can I go now?" Dr. Maudlin said to Dr. Delight as they nibbled salads in the physicians' dining room the next day. "Neither science, nor philosophy nor religion have helped."

"Where do you usually go when you have a serious question?"

"My lawyer. But what do lawyers know about death?"

"He must know something, Lewis. You paid him enough for your estate plan."

So late that afternoon, Dr. Maudlin met Solway Page in an office larger than the pathology laboratory at the hospital. At the lawyer's hourly rate, it was better for Maudlin to go to his office than to invite him to the hospital, where a traffic jam could cost the doctor thousands of dollars.

"How do you know you're dead?" the lawyer repeated, opening Dr. Maudlin's file and pushing a paper across the desk. "Just look at your obituary. Didn't you see it?"

Lewis Maudlin was surprised to see his face at the top of three column inches describing a meteoric career in medicine and marriage that ended with the highest professional honors and enough children to support several private schools and colleges.

"Is this a joke?" he said.

"In the legal profession we never joke. Here's the order admitting your will to probate, and here are copies of my letters to the beneficiaries. You'll be happy to know that everything is going according to plan." The lawyer paused. "Is something the matter?"

"I just can't believe it."

"It must have been quite a shock. They said they found you slumped over the obituary page on your breakfast table."

"Was there an autopsy?"

Page showed him another paper. Dr. Maudlin recognised Dr. Blinder's signature and the final diagnosis: acute myocardial infarction.

"It has to be a mistake."

"I was at the memorial service, Lewis. And at the internment."

"How could I have missed my own memorial service?"

"Beats hell out of me. Maybe because you were cremated beforehand."

"How am I going to get my prescriptions refilled?" Maudlin exclaimed. "Or pay for anything with my credit card?"

"Just take it easy. It usually takes some time for people to realise what's happened. I'll make sure the estate pays all reasonable expenses."

"I can't live with this, Solly. You have to turn it around."

"No way, Doctor. The law moves slowly, but once it acts, it's over. Even the Supreme Court can't bring you legally back to life."

The lawyer had never seen his client so distressed.

"It was a bad week for the hospital," he continued to divert the doctor from his problems. "Did you see that young pathologist with the funny name, Delight I think it was, got killed in a traffic accident on her way to the sports medicine gala last Saturday?"

Lewis Maudlin's head sank forward. He was crying.

"Can I get you a drink?" the lawyer offered, and without waiting for a reply, poured each of them a shot from a bottle on his credenza. "Don't take it so hard, buddy. It happens to a lot of people."

"The girl," Maudlin said. "I knew her."

"I'm sorry."

Lewis Maudlin swirled the whiskey in his glass until it was at body temperature. It had been a long time since he had enjoyed the taste of good bourbon. With each sip he was gradually enveloped by a feeling of warmth and comfort, and his problems seemed more and more manageable. When he got home, he would call Christie and see what she was doing that evening, he thought.

When Solway Graham walked him out of his office, Dr. Maudlin even smiled at the lawyer's administrative assistant and the two associates who were standing by her desk, waiting their turn with the great man.

"Be sure to take some time for yourself, Lew," the lawyer said as they parted. "For some people this is a very big event."

"Why is it that we have to go to lawyers to learn the most basic facts about ourselves?" Dr. Maudlin said as he lifted another slice of pizza from the box onto his plate.

Christie seemed withdrawn, as if his brashness from the bourbon had unsettled her. Although she had specified the chicken and Parmesan cheese topping, she had hardly eaten a bite.

"Are you alright?" he asked her.

"I went to my memorial service this afternoon," she said slowly. "Maybe I should have stayed home."

"What happened?"

"My parents and sister were there."

She was crying. Maudlin set down his pizza and reached for her hand.

"I'm sorry."

"That's OK. I'll get over it."

Maudlin was not so sure. She had not met his eyes all evening.

"Look, Christie. Maybe we should get away for awhile. What about one of those river boat cruises in Europe or a trip to China?"

"They were starting to clean out my apartment when I came over here."

She's still thinking about her family, Dr. Maudlin thought.

"You really don't have anyone, do you, Lewis?"

"No," he said. "Except you."

"Maybe that makes it easier."

"Aren't you going to have any of your pizza?"

"Let's go outside."

His condo was on the twenty-third floor of a spectacular development overlooking the downtown and the river. Toward the West, where the river curled out of sight, the sun was setting in a dazzling orange summer sky. As he slid open the glass doors to the balcony, the late summer air, sweet and moist, surrounded them.

"It hurts to leave all this, but I have to," she said, facing him.

"You knew it all along, didn't you?"

She smiled.

"Why didn't you tell me?"

"It was just so funny seeing you trying to figure it out as if you were still a surgeon."

"And now?"

"You have to make up your own mind what to do now, Lewis."

She kissed him and stepped back.

"I wish we could have met another way, Christie."

She climbed up onto the balcony rail as lightly as a gymnast and balanced there, arms outstretched, her head blocking the sun.

"Good bye, Dr. Maudlin," she said and faded off into the evening sky.

Reaching after her, Lewis Maudlin climbed onto the rail.

For a second he hesitated, trying to think of a question the lawyer could not answer. Before he could frame it, he knew the answer and let go.

***

Dear Violet
Lucy Brown

Lucy Brown is a freelance writer and academic from Yorkshire who particularly enjoys writing on LGBT themes. She has several publishing credits including recently published essays on television dramas such as *Downton Abbey* and *Call the Midwife*. 2015 has been a busy year which saw her being shortlisted in Aestas 2015 and winning the Dickens Journals Online Literary Journalism Competition, apart from getting her PhD at the University of Sheffield.

Judge Leela Panikar says about *Dear Violet* "The intriguing first paragraph invites the reader in immediately. There is a certain amount of mystery which is well handled. Tightly written, with great dialogues and no rambling, this is the art of short story writing."

Nothing stirred in the kitchen. Hands cupped into the flecked filth of the back window, Di peered inside. The walls were slathered with yellow, sunshine soured over the years to glisten like urine instead. In places it had flaked off entirely, puckering the room with gnarled eyeballs that ogled the stained linoleum and chipped worktops. Deflated, Di stepped away onto the slab of weeds that passed as the lawn, scrubbing her hands on her jeans.

A figure loomed out of the gloom of the hallway. It shuffled along from the direction of the stairs, chin dipped and arms splayed out against the walls on either side. Grey hair sheared short, it was only recognisable as a woman by the swollen skirt swaying as she moved. When she shambled into a shaft of sunlight filtering through the grimy glass her unseeing eyes glittered and the unsightly kitchen suddenly made sense. Di hesitated on the lawn, torn between her purpose and leaving this woman in peace. A day wasted, a train journey paid for out of her own pocket – they were considerations, but it was the faint kindling of hope that prompted her to return to the back door and knock again. After a moment, the door opened and the woman's chin appeared against the chain.

'Who is it?' she asked, voice as bedraggled as her hair.

'My name's Diane Crowther,' she replied. 'You don't know me. I…' Trailing off, she flushed, almost relieved the woman couldn't see her face.

'What is it, love?' the woman pressed. 'You're not from 'round here. I can tell from your voice.'

'Not far,' she answered, scuffing her foot against the step. 'Derbyshire.'

'Ha,' she said with a chortle, 'practically another country then. What is it you're after?'

Di crossed her arms and cleared her throat. 'This is going to sound so stupid and I know since you sent the letter back you probably haven't got a clue. I wouldn't have bothered if I'd known about your . . . your eyesight, it's too much of an imposition, but

I'm here now and . . .' She shook her babble away and forced the question out: 'Does the name Violet Stree mean anything to you?'

The woman buckled, jamming her shoulder against the sliver of wall visible through the crack.

'You've heard the name then?' Di questioned. 'Did she live here before you? Did you know her?'

'I am her,' the woman murmured. 'A long time since anyone called me it though.'

Di frowned. 'No, the electoral register says Cynthia Coe lives here.'

'I'm Cynthia now,' she said, 'but I was Violet for a while, only a little while. Before that I was Cynthia.'

'But I don't . . .' With questions swarming in her head she plucked out the simplest: 'Well, what do I call you?'

A knobbly hand gripped the door frame. 'Depends on why you're here, doesn't it? Who did you say you were?'

'Diane,' she said. 'I've got a letter for Violet. Can I come in?'

-

The sink was encrusted with lime scale and the kettle was much the same. Di washed two cups with tepid water and wiped them off with kitchen roll then made tea and joined the woman in the living room, nearly stumbling over the threadbare trenches in the carpet.

'Watch out for the carpet,' the woman called. 'It's not all that level.'

A radio buzzed out classical music in the corner, echoing around the austere room. When Di placed the cups on the table between the two armchairs the woman raised her head.

'You can call me Violet,' she said. 'Since you're here about that, it's only right. Could you turn the radio off?'

The silence settled over the room. Di perched on the edge of the second armchair, keeping her elbows clear of the blackened blotches of food and drink that littered the upholstery.

'You said you've got a letter,' Violet prompted.

Di tucked her hand into her bag. 'Do you remember – you might not have heard it – last year a post box that hadn't been emptied for nearly forty years was found?'

Violet stiffened, her hands clawing at each other. 'How long?'

'Between thirty eight and nine years.'

'So it's not recent, this letter?' Violet questioned. 'It's not from her nephew or anything like that?'

'No,' Di replied, 'it's from Rose.'

'And it was written when?' she asked finally, bony fingers tying themselves in knots.

'April 1979,' said Di.

Violet let out a whimper. 'The April, it says it's the April?'

Hand closing over the letter, Di tugged it out of her bag. 'Do you want me to read it to you?'

'I don't think I could hear it just now,' Violet murmured. 'Not yet. Something like this takes some adjusting to after all this time.' Her hands settled on her lap. 'You've read it.'

'Yes,' Di admitted. 'We tried to reunite the letters and postcards with their owners, their addressees where possible, the sender if not. We sent it here, but it was returned unopened.'

'My son, I bet,' Violet said. 'He wouldn't know and he deals with everything like that these days. He looks after me since I lost my sight altogether.'

'You weren't always blind then?' she asked, then she could've kicked herself.

Violet half-smiled. 'Don't be embarrassed.'

Stiffening, Di muttered, 'How did you know?'

'You pick up on it,' replied Violet with a shrug. 'Inflection, tone, volume, even the words you use. Some reckon it compensates, but I don't buy that. No,' she went on, 'my sight was damaged after an accident and it went downhill from there. I've been like this for six years, round about. It takes some getting used to. Where was it?' she questioned. 'This post box.'

'Near the station at Derby,' Di answered, falling into the spiel she'd been peddling for months now. 'It was ignored for a while, forgotten about. There were renovations nearby in the mid-seventies. A burst water pipe started it off and they did a bit of sprucing up. The post box would've been a bit off the beaten track when they were done, and it was out of commission for a few months.

'Round about then – though we can't level up the dates exactly – there was a bit of a scandal with a postman. He was using postcards sent back by people on their holidays to burgle their houses,' she explained. 'Or, at least, he was putting the information in the way of those who would burgle them. He was sacked, went to prison for a bit, and it's likely the box was just forgotten about. When it reopened – when it should've reopened – it was just missed from the rounds. People continued putting letters in it, but, like I said, it was a bit off the beaten track so it was never that many. It only filled to the brim last year, someone put in a complaint and . . . here we are. I'm sorry,' she said, 'are you all right?'

A tear dribbled along the wrinkles in Violet's cheek. 'Fate, call it fate.'

Di resisted the urge to take her hand. 'I can see why you'd think that.'

'What other way is there to think about it?' Violet questioned. 'She got off the train in Derby – she wasn't meant to do that. So she gets off the train somewhere unexpected and she puts a letter into a box that's out of use. How can you not see the hand of God in that?'

'Are you religious?' asked Di.

'I wasn't.' She paused. 'Now I wonder.'

'It doesn't explain what she was doing in Derby, the letter,' Di went on after a moment. 'But it does look like it was written in a hurry, maybe even on the train if some of the writing's anything to go by.'

'It's not neat? She was always so neat, with flourishes. Like flowers on the page,' Violet added, 'that's what I used to say about it.'

'Jagged, maybe that's the word,' Di replied. 'Coupled with what she says, I think she got off the train especially to post it to you.'

For a minute Violet was silent. Then she murmured, 'She never wrote again.'

'No,' said Di, 'she wouldn't have.'

Drawing herself up abruptly, Violet groped her way to the windowsill, tilting her face towards the sun. 'Let me – let me . . . What must you think of me? After what I . . . then I let her down as well.'

'I don't see how that's the case,' Di answered. 'Fate – that's more like it, like you said before. Accident, that's all.'

'What I did wasn't accidental,' returned Violet. 'The only way I've coped is to forget it. Now I feel guilty about that. It wasn't planned,' she rushed on. 'I didn't even know it was happening – nor did she. We worked together at the library for a long while then one day . . .'

When she trailed off, Di felt compelled to say, 'You don't have to tell me.'

Violet chuckled and pressed a hand to the glass. 'I've never told anybody,' she muttered. 'Maybe it's about time I did.'

'Okay,' Di answered, knitting her arms together.

'Like I say,' Violet continued after shuffling back to her armchair, 'we worked together. We were friends, not so much away from work, though I didn't notice it much at the time. She didn't know my Alan very well and she wasn't married. But we never really talked about any of that. We talked about books and what was going on in the world. Back then, there was plenty. It was all things that Alan never thought I'd want to talk about. I suppose that's how it started.

'I could never tell you when it changed,' she went on. 'But I know when I realised. They were making some people redundant across the board, asking for volunteers. Alan had been promoted by then and he was earning enough so that I didn't have to work if I minded it. I didn't want to leave, Rose didn't want me to leave and it hit us both I reckon. We still didn't talk about it, of course. It was like Pandora's Box, we were too scared of opening it, where it might lead. Then it came to a head. It always does, I suppose.'

Di had been overtly staring in a way she wouldn't have dared if Violet could see her. Every twitch of unease and regret had seized her attention, though love was the most obvious thing. It oozed from every word trembling from her lips. To think that she'd suppressed this – ignored it, forgotten it – for over thirty years was incomprehensible.

'Anyway,' Violet continued after finding her cup and taking a sip of tea, 'I twisted my ankle falling off a step-ladder. She looked after me, so caring with it, and I gave in. I thought I couldn't fight it. I was wrong, I'm sure I must've been wrong.'

Though she could understand why she felt compelled to say it, Di knew it was a lie.

Violet flattened her palms against her knees. 'She was proud,' she said. 'She was quicker off the mark accepting it and she wouldn't be on the outside. I was so swept up in it that I agreed. I agreed to leave Alan, to leave my son – though he was already out of school and working. I said I'd go, that we'd make the best of it somewhere else. She'd go on ahead of me and get a job. We were thinking Cornwall. She'd write and I'd join her, only she never did. Read it me,' she added suddenly. 'Could you read it me?'

Though she could recite it by now, Di slid the letter out from the envelope, the paper coarse against her fingertips.

'Dear Violet,' she read. 'I wanted to put this in writing because I don't think I made it clear when we last spoke. You see, I was swept away with the fantasy and I lost sight of the reality we live in. Please don't think I'm taking anything back. I'm not. But I have nothing to lose and you have everything, you see. I don't know that I could make it worth your while, I doubt I could ever be enough to make up for all the guilt you'll have. Would it be worth it if you began to hate me and hate yourself? How could I want that?

'I'm not going to Cornwall, I've changed my mind. I'm going to stay with my brother in Blackpool instead, you've got the address. Write to me there if you still want to go ahead, but give it time, months instead of weeks. I won't be angry if the days pass by and I never hear from you. I'll know you made the right choice for you and I'll respect that because, above all, you want the person you love to be happy. If I never hear from you I'll treasure our time together and I won't yearn for anything more. If that's how our story ends then so be it. For the last three years, knowing you, I've felt like myself. And you, I hope, have felt very much like Violet. All my love, Rose.'

As Di folded the letter back up, she looked away from the tears drizzling along Violet's cheeks.

'You didn't let her down,' she said when the tears had subsided. 'I think you were right – I think it was fate.'

'I've been happy,' murmured Violet, fumbling for a tissue, 'but was she?'

'I don't know,' Di answered. 'Can you ask her now?'

'She died,' was the soft reply. 'I checked year after year on what would've been her birthday, the one time I let myself think about it. She died in Lancashire nine years ago, ten this May. Some sort of cancer, they weren't specific.'

Di slumped back into the dirty chair. Eventually, she asked, 'Would you have been better not knowing?'

Violet's head snapped up. 'You've brought me the final chapter, you've closed the book. After all this time, knowing she'd have forgiven me for not going, even if I had got the letter . . . That's a gift, you don't know how much of one. You don't know what you've done for me.'

Reaching across, Di took a quivering hand in her own. 'I'm beginning to,' she said.

***

Last Prayers at the Chapel

Hannah Persaud

Hannah Persaud was born in Yorkshire, England, and grew up in Kathmandu, Nepal, before going to school in India. She returned to England to complete her studies, and graduated with an English degree from Oxford Brookes University. Pursuing her childhood dream of becoming a writer, Hannah has won and been placed in a number of short story and poetry competitions. Currently, she is working on her first novel.

Last Prayers at the Chapel is the only horror story in this collection. We loved the way it unfolded, and the twist at the very end. Judge Anisha Bhaduri sums it up best "making readers believe the unbelievable is not easy. It is even more difficult getting them to believe what the writer wants them to. A reader mustn't know that the words in black shouldn't be believed and the writer must not let out that it is not really about believing what one reads. It is a tight contest, and Hannah Persaud wins easily."

The postman comes just as Tom is leaving the house. On a normal day he would fling the pile onto the counter and leave them for Charlotte to sort through, but when he spots the A4 envelope with the estate agent's logo on, he siphons it away from the others and slides it into his briefcase. It wouldn't do for Charlotte to stumble across this one by accident.

The day blends into a whirl of meetings, sweaty tube journeys and heated phone calls, and an awkward team meeting leaves Tom frustrated. He seeks solace in a pint with Michael on the way home.

'Are you seriously thinking about leaving?' Michael downs the dregs of his beer in one swallow. 'Another?' Tom looks at his watch, it's getting late, he should be getting home.

'All right then, just one more.' They drink the next ones slower. 'Freelancing is the way forward mate, independence, pick and choose what you work on, the comfort of your own home.' Tom rubs his hands together.

'Could get lonely though, no office, no workplace gossip.' Michael looks with concern at Tom whose eyes have glazed over. 'I know it's been hard for you recently but… you won't have much company…'

'Exactly, sounds perfect to me. Just get the work done and leave all the bureaucracy behind. Work to live not live to work. I'm not getting any younger you know.' He pats his stomach which paunches out over his belt.

'You'd better invite us down, if you do go for it. Miriam would love it too – a break from the city, a slice of country life. She'll be nagging me to do the same before you know it.' Tom nods, puts his empty glass on the table beside the faded beer mat.

'Course we would, you know Charlotte loves you guys.' Michael nods uncomfortably.

'It's about time you had a change of scene, Miriam says it will do you good.' Michael pats him on the shoulder.

-

It's gone 11pm by the time he walks through their gate. The only light on in the house glows through their bedroom window. He's left it far too late to do the sales pitch tonight, the intimate dinner and bottle of wine over candlelight slipped away as the beer in the Kings Head ran down his throat. He'll be lucky if she's even talking to him.

'You forgot to phone.' Charlotte's lying in bed on her side, book propped up on her pillow. She doesn't turn when he walks in. Leaning down he tries to kiss her mouth but she turns her head and he catches her ear, a whiff of Davidoff.

'Sorry darling, crazy day, I lost track of time. Saw Michael on the way home, he sends his love.' She puts her bookmark in the page and turns off the reading light, plunging Tom into darkness. He stumbles over the end of the bed on his way to the bathroom. 'I'll make it up to you tomorrow, I promise.' She sighs as his attempts to close the bathroom door quietly are thwarted by him crashing into the shower door and knocking off the shower gels.

'I got my period today,' she mumbles as he climbs into bed. He pulls her into his arms and falls asleep as he counts the number of months they've been trying for a baby.

Plans for the next evening go better, he's left work early to buy the ingredients for the Thai curry, picked up a couple of bottles of her favourite Viognier. By the time she gets home from work, the food will be cooking and they can have a glass of wine on the patio. Perfect. Only one minor thing bothers him; a tiny detail but one that will likely topple his entire dream like a row of dominoes. Charlotte is superstitious. The possibility that she would give up their modern town house in Chiswick to convert an old chapel in a remote Cotswold village is quite frankly ludicrous. He knows it, and fairly soon she will know it too. But Tom is nothing if not an optimist, and he's promised himself one fair shot at persuading her, because this could be the beginning of the everything else that they have always talked about. His recent inheritance could buy the property outright and pay for all the renovations, leaving money left over to invest into setting up his own company. It would mean that Charlotte could leave her job that she loathes too. He wouldn't have dreamt of making such a move if it wasn't for Charlotte deciding to write a book.

'Just think, if I get it published we could live anywhere, we won't need to be tied to London for my job. No more commuting, no more rubbing shoulders with sweaty tourists or standing freezing on platforms.' He'd laughed at the time, but with her first draft complete and her dedication to the book dwarfing her enthusiasm for anything else, he's realised that she could be right. This could be the perfect time for a change.

–

He's standing on the doorstep leaning against the door and rummaging through the shopping bag looking for the lemon grass, when the door flies open and he falls into the hall. Oyster mushrooms and lime leaves scatter and one of the two bottles of Viognier smashes. Wine splurges across their heated concrete floor.

'What are you doing here?'

'What are you doing here more like?' Charlotte bends to pick up the elusive lemon grass.

'It was supposed to be a surprise, for you.' Recovering himself with dignity proves difficult whilst standing in a puddle of wine.

Half an hour later and the delicate aromas of Thai curry waft gently through their house, the remaining bottle of wine is decanted out into a carafe and they sit on their patio bathed in the orange plumes of the setting sun. Tom's hand drops to the envelope that he has put on the floor beside him, and as their talk turns to plans for the approaching winter he slides the contents across the table. Charlotte looks at him.

'Another surprise?'

'Sort of.' He clears his throat. 'What do you think?' The silence whilst she scans the first page, then the second, is almost unbearable, yet he almost hopes for it to not be broken, for whilst it is intact so is the dream. Scraping back her chair from the table, Charlotte stands and moves behind him, wraps her arms around his neck and places her face against his.

'I love it. When do we go and see it?'

-

It is a beautiful drive and the weather could not be better as they wind their way through the narrow country lanes flanked with high hedges – skylarks and buzzards circle the sky above and the whole land is soaked in a golden hue. A breeze whips their hair through the open windows and Charlotte has tied hers up with a scarf.

'I feel like Bridget Jones' she laughs. Guiting Power nestles on a hillside, a small place for such a grand title.

'Guiting means fast flowing. There's a stream that flows through the village from an earth dam.' The estate agent points to the bottom of the valley where the trees thicken. The estate agent is impressing Charlotte, Tom can tell, despite her loathing of them. She'd not even commented on the branding on his car when he'd pulled up. *Connecting people with property.* The chapel is small and square, perching on the edge of the hillside before it drops away. Its Cotswold stone sits comfortably in the landscape and the arched windows are in fairly good condition with only a couple of panes of glass missing. Whilst they are waiting for the agent Tom scrambles up the bank to the high walls and peeks over. Even by his standards this might be pushing it a bit. Having a graveyard in your garden is one thing – having your house in the middle of a graveyard quite another.

'Goodness, the tombstones are right up against the house' whispers Charlotte as they are led in through the front gate. No word of a lie in that statement. Tom glances at her to catch her expression. To his surprise there's no hint of a frown, no hesitation in the way she moves eagerly to the front door. Inside her enthusiasm continues, matched by the estate agent's as he insists on telling them the history of the place.

'First it was a schoolhouse, then a chapel. It fell into disrepair but a wealthy landowner poured money into restoring it in the early 1900s. Closing down all over the country they are now, these chapels with small congregations. Such a shame.' Even his sigh seems to have a west country accent.

'Look.' Charlotte gestures from the window. Tom follows her finger to where she is pointing, one of the larger graves has fresh flowers on it.

'Ah yes.' The estate agent rubs his forehead. 'That's the only other thing, the graveyard is, well, it's attended.'

'Attended?' For the first time Tom hears doubt in Charlotte's voice.

'Attended by whom?' Tom asks.

'Well, the families of the, uh, dead people. That is, the people who visit the graves. The people who buy this chapel have to ensure that they still have access to visit.' Tom paces in circles, avoids looking at Charlotte.

'Are you telling me that you have dragged me all the way down here from London to look at living in the middle of an active graveyard, yet you omitted to mention this until now?' The agent lowers his head, clears his throat.

'I am sure I..'

'Not *active*, darling, *attended*. Quite a difference I'd say wouldn't you?' Charlotte smiles at him brightly, not a cloud in her eyes.

Moving day comes quickly, being chain free has released all brakes. Any moment now she's going to flip, he knows it. It's all been too good to be true, Charlotte has not been deterred by anything since the moment they laid eyes on the chapel.

'It's nuts,' he'd said to Michael at his leaving do. 'It's as if she was never superstitious at all. There's a gravestone literally pushing up against the wall of what will be our kitchen, it'll be the first thing she sees in the morning when she opens the curtains, the last thing she sees at night. And she's no more concerned about it then if it were a flowerpot.'

'Sounds to me old man like you're the one with the jitters.' Michael laughed, and handed him another beer.

'I'm not superstitious, just practical – you can't even get to the door of the chapel without winding your way between the stones.'

'If you're having doubts mate, better to change your mind now than when it's too late.'

'She'd never forgive me if I bailed out now, after all, the whole thing was my idea. It's as if she's had fresh air blown into her.'

The caravan they've hired is small and creaky and at night the draught whistles through the length of it. Tom shivers whilst Charlotte sleeps deeply. It was all a part of their plan, to live in a caravan whilst they did the place up, just…he hadn't imagined that the caravan would be in the corner of the graveyard.

'It's the only place for it love' Charlotte had insisted, 'the only other option is to have it on the road, and then we'll get into all sorts of trouble with the highways agency, plus the neighbours will have a field day'. The neighbours are already having a field day, he pointed out, he'd seen them peering over the edge of the wall and heard them whispering in the village shop. 'Nonsense' she'd said, 'it's only natural that they'll talk about us for a while, any outsider takes time to settle in.' She doesn't appear to feel lonely at all, but he is. Working for himself is hard, as Michael said it would be, and between networking by day and working on the chapel in the evenings, he's never known such exhaustion. They haven't made love since they left London, and Charlotte doesn't seem to have noticed. Not that a creaky caravan with a view of headstones is the most seductive of environments anyway.

-

It has taken them six months to finish the conversion and the results are stunning. The simple chapel has been transformed inside, they've kept the paving stone floor with its worn away stones at the entrance, and restored the iron edged windows. The ceiling vaults above them, amplifying the Ludovico Einaudi album that Charlotte has selected. They're sitting on the only second story level in the building, *the sanctuary*, Charlotte calls it. They've stripped back the wooden floors and created a mezzanine level, a leather sofa and coffee table sit on a cow-hide and at this time of day the light filters through the windows, casting shadows on the walls.

'We did it' Charlotte clinks her glass to his. 'I can't believe this is all ours.' Tom smiles, forcing his tired eyes to focus on hers.

'We did indeed darling, our very own slice of rural life.'

'Tom?'

'Yes darling?'

'I know you said you wanted Michael and Miriam down to visit, but can we postpone it just a little bit longer? I just wanted to keep this to ourselves, just a little while more.' He's been putting them off for weeks.

'I guess a few more weeks won't hurt anyone'. He strokes the back of her hair, notes the hollows under her eyes. They are both exhausted, she's been working on her novel constantly since they moved out of the caravan. Perhaps it would be better to wait until they've caught up on some sleep.

-

His business has really taken off, and he's finding himself travelling more and more away from their new home.

'I'm sorry Charlotte, this is only temporary.' A few years ago she would have shuddered at the idea of a night alone, even in their brand new house.

'It's fine, I know you need to build it up, I'm fine here, honestly.' And she is. Every time he phones her when he is away, she sounds bright, happy, always busy and occupied.

'I'm just tidying up the hallway.'

'I'd better go, I'm expecting a delivery'.

'I need to tidy up the graveyard before it rains.' He's been in London for four days and is missing her warmth beside him, the meeting of tomorrow has been cancelled and he's decided he's going to surprise her by turning up unannounced. Plus there is something that needs celebrating; he found the pregnancy test in the bathroom bin just before he came on this trip.

The chapel is in darkness as he parks on the road, but it's late and she could well be in bed already. He lets himself in quietly through the front gate, shines his phone torch to see his way between the gravestones. Something is different. He looks around. The stones glow in the reflected light of his torch, the lettering decipherable for the first time since they moved here. The grass around them is neat and fresh flowers adorn the graves. An owl calls and Tom shivers in a sudden breeze. He moves around the corner of the chapel slowly, to where the land dips down towards the wooded valley. She's cleaned them all up, each and every one, even the stones that lean against the back of the chapel, stones whose bodies have been moved elsewhere. It must have taken her hours, days. Returning to the front door, he unlocks it, or rather, tries to, but the key won't turn. It is already unlocked. He must have a word with her about safety, rural setting or not. In the kitchen he moves to the fridge and pours himself a glass of wine.

'Charlotte?' Somewhere in the darkened living room something drops on the floor and a sound like a child's laughter bounces off the ceiling. It must be the bats that are living in the rafters. Flicking a light on he sees a post it note on the floor beneath the notice board, a pin beside it. Pinning it back up he moves towards the back of the chapel, where the altar is. On the dining table is a pile of papers. It is an unspoken rule that he doesn't read her writing unless she asks him to. He turns to survey the room and then he realises what is different. The room is warm. So warm that he is sweating beneath his suit. The chapel is always cold, its thick walls cooling the air inside. Even with the heating on they walk around with layers on. Tom looks at the room and then to the windows. The glass on the windows is fogged up, condensation is dripping from the panes. Not just one, but all of the windows, all the way up to the roof top. As if the room were full of hot warm bodies. In spite of the heat, he pulls his jacket closer.

'Charlotte?' louder now, he pushes through to the bedroom, turns the lights on to find the room still and the bed bare. He lifts the home phone and is in the middle of dialling the number of their closest neighbour, when the front door slams and Charlotte comes in, barefoot and her hair wild across her back.

'Where have you been?' He shouts rarely, but she does not seem surprised. 'I was outside, finishing the weeding.'

'Liar.' The word is out before he can stop it. Her cheeks flush and she walks closer.

'What are you doing here anyway? You're supposed to be in London.'

'I came back early, to see you.'

'Well you shouldn't have.' Her feet leave damp marks on the floor as she walks away. This is not the homecoming he'd imagined, but he's too angry to follow. By the time she comes back he is in the midst of half sleep and he feels her cool body against his back as she slides beneath the covers. In the morning he remembers her secret and softens slightly, he will let her tell him when she is ready.

That weekend Michael and Miriam visit.

'You weren't exaggerating when you described this place, it's beautiful, but what a project to take on.' Michael steps back to look at the ceiling that throws a crocheted pattern of rafters through the dust flecked light.

'I'm not sure many people would have gone for it Tom.' Miriam nudged his elbow playfully. Kudos to you for doing so though.' Although he has missed them, their visit feels strained. He catches Charlotte's eye during dinner, doesn't recognise what she is trying to tell him. She's barely said a word since they arrived. He awakes in the night to find Miriam kneeling in the lounge with her hand upon the altar.

'I heard something, a footstep'.

'It's just the nature of this place, it creaks and groans.'

She looks at him doubtfully.

'It was running, a fast pitter patter, like a child's.'

'You should be the one writing the book.' He grins at her before heading back to bed. It is with relief that he waves them off on Sunday.

'I'm sorry about Charlotte, she's going through a difficult time.' Miriam looks at her feet as Michael hugs him. Charlotte has not come out, pleading a headache – their warm chatter and funny anecdotes felt clumsy and out of place this time.

'You could have made more effort' he says to Charlotte later, 'I wasn't asking much, one visit in 10 months, it's not much to ask.' She shrugs and turns away.

–

Tom is fed up of working for himself now. He's been camped out in a hotel for the past five days. Things have gone from bad to worse with Charlotte. The lost baby has made everything worse. The timing was awful. One Sunday, when he couldn't bear the not knowing any longer, he broached the subject of the pregnancy test he had found. She had nodded; yes, she was; yes she had wanted to keep it a surprise; yes he would be a father. Then, just hours after that conversation, she'd lost the baby. If she was upset, he was devastated. And he wasn't even sure she was that upset, given that the very same evening, instead of staying inside with him and mourning together, she'd gone back out to the graveyard where she spent more and more time and sat there amongst the stones, whispering to herself.

He hasn't seen or heard from Michael for weeks now, not since their visit. He's got a feeling that Michael's been ignoring his calls. Driving back from Brighton he feels as if it is years, not days, since he last saw Charlotte. He didn't bother to phone her this time whilst he was away. Perhaps some space would be good for them. As soon as he rounds the corner he can see that something is not right. It's the middle of the afternoon and the front gate is open, the front door too. From inside he can hear singing. Before he has even got his right foot onto the pavement, a woman he recognises from the tittering gossips in the shop besieges him.

'Thank the lord you're back, oh it's been a terrible thing, we've all been so worried.'

'What has? Worried about what?' he shifts restlessly, he doesn't have time for this right now.

'Come. Have a look.' She leads him up the bank and

stands on her tiptoes as he once did when he first came to visit the chapel. He looks over the wall, and then he sees it. The two headstones closest to the gate are desecrated; graffiti sprawled across their inscriptions. Beneath each one lies a mound of loose earth; where the coffin should have lain, a hole.

'We don't know if its vandals or what, we've been so frightened. It's not the first time it's happened, though that was before your time. We're so glad you're home to sort it out.'

'Why didn't you ask Charlotte to call me?' He finally manages to interrupt the woman's chatter. She looks at him strangely. 'She's around all day, why didn't you ask her to sort it out?' At this, she steps backwards, almost falling down the bank. That's it. He's had enough. Walking back around the wall Tom marches through the gate and open front door, into the cold worn slate hallway where the stones sit unevenly. The singing grows louder, and he waits, hand on the door that leads to the lounge. As he turns the handle, the singing stops abruptly and he hears a distinct clattering of wood against stone. Flinging the door open he catches a glimpse of rows of wooden benches, a bible slipping from the seat to the floor as if hastily dropped. Raising his eyes to the ceiling it feels for a moment that the sky is falling inwards, the shards of light blinding. Rubbing stars from his eyes he opens them again to the room that he stands in. His lounge, just as it has been since they moved in, and there, on the altar at the back of the room, his Charlotte, seated at the table, immersed in her writing. She looks up as he approaches, gives him a wry smile as she rises and folds herself into his arms.

'Thank god you're okay' he mumbles into her hair, her soft skin. She can explain everything later.

'They were prayers for the souls of the dead.' She leans back in his arms. A chill runs down his back.

'What were?'

'Those songs that you heard.' A jumble of voices from the doorway reach him, he feels a flash of anger at being disturbed at this moment when he finally has his Charlotte in his arms.

'I told him…..and he said I should have…'

'It's not the first time this has happened…it wasn't his fault' – the voice is familiar. Turning, he sees the woman from outside, and Michael.

'Tom, listen to me, you need to let me go.' She holds his face between her hands.

'No, Charlotte, you don't understand, I want to be with you, I do.' She shakes her head sadly. 'I belong here Tom.'

'Tom, come on mate, come here for a minute.' Michael beckons from the door. Tom looks at Charlotte and she nods, squeezes his hand before he walks away.

-

After the police have left, and the neighbours have been placated, Tom sits across from Michael in the pub down the road.

'Look mate, I love you to bits, but you need to sort yourself out, you can't carry on this way.' Tom stares at Michael.

'How could some random grave diggers possibly be my fault? Yes I could have been around more, but that doesn't excuse the fact that this is the work of vandals. I knew I should have had CCTV fitted. It's first on the list to do tomorrow.'

'It's not that mate, it's… look, there's this guy, he's really good, treated a friend of my dad's after his wife died. I think you should see him.' He presses a business card into the palm of Tom's hand. Tom stares blankly at it.

'We should have known it was a bad idea, you moving out to here to be with the family graves. We understood you wanting to be close to Charlotte, but it's just been too much for you.'

'What do you mean, close to Charlotte?'

'Come on mate, we've indulged you for almost two years now, but you need to move on. You can't pretend that you didn't know that this is where she was buried.' Buried. The word burrows into his head like a worm.

'It wasn't your fault, her body wasn't strong enough to survive the birth, the baby wasn't either. Nobody could have predicted what would happen, you did everything you could.' And suddenly, through the fog of the beer and his exhaustion, Tom does remember. His hand on her swollen stomach at night, the planning, hoping, dreaming. And then, too soon, the hot fluorescent lights, the silver scalpel's edge against soft flesh. A flash of searing love for his tiny daughter with her perfect half moon fingernails who joined this world too fleetingly before departing. Taking his Charlotte with her. The time before the pain came.

Outside the pub, Michael throws his arm around Tom's shoulder.

'I'm going to stay here tonight, then tomorrow you're going to come back up to London with me for a while, ok? Take a break, get some rest. You look exhausted.' Tom nods, head bowed.

Michael settles himself in the lounge and Tom is outside about to lock up, when something in the corner of the graveyard catches his eye. It's right beside where the caravan was, would have been concealed by it. Walking over he bends down in front of the stone that he has not noticed before, shines his torch on it.

Lilian Rose Mayhew

Beloved Daughter of Charlotte and Tom

Taken too soon

Born and Died, 29th November, 2012

Buried here with her mother Charlotte Mayhew

Forever holding hands

Kneeling down on the damp grass he folds himself to the ground, rests his forehead against the grave, and weeps.

-

Before he turns the lights out in the lounge, he sees the draft manuscript of Charlotte's novel still upon the table. It will never be published. It is time to put it away. As he picks up the papers he glances again at the handwriting that sprawls across the top sheet, notices a new line in red pen. *Darling Tom, thank for you for bringing me home to rest. Now it's your turn. Yours, Charlotte.*

***

First Kill

Timothy O'Leary

Born in Billings, USA, Timothy O'Leary enjoyed a long career in television and advertising before becoming a full-time writer in 2014. He was a finalist for the 2015 Mississippi Review Prize and Washington Square Review fiction awards, and the Mark Twain Royal Nonesuch Humor award. His work has been published or is forthcoming in Lost River Review, Fabula Argentea, Heater, Talking River, the anthologies *And All Our Yesterdays*, *Theatre B*, *The Water Holds no Scars*, and many other publications. He received his MFA from Pacific University, and resides outside of Portland, USA. More information on Timothy is available at www.timothyolearylit.com.

Judge Clare Wallace says of *First Kill* "this was just a joy to read. It was, as much great fiction is, a fantastic example of escapism and of daring to do the thing we shouldn't. The sense of place was fully realised and the characterisation unique, astute, and completely believable while still challenging preconceptions. As the short story format goes, I felt that this was excellently formed, and completely satisfying."

On Friday night Justin's father arrived home unexpectedly. Justin's mom, always mysteriously thrilled to see the man, rushed to prepare an alternative to the cuisine she'd planned; the McDonalds filet-o-fish and fries replaced with iceberg lettuce and carrots drenched in Green Goddess, and a main course of stringy pasta with venison meatballs, served all fancy with a bottle of Two Buck Chuck and a bag of Famous Amos for dessert. She even brought out the shiny white china she'd collected one piece at a time with every twenty-five-dollar purchase at Safeway, using a metal mixing bowl for the sauce, since she hadn't spent enough to collect the serving dishes. Justin seriously doubted she'd ever own the entire set, unless Mickey D's and Jack in the Box participated in the promotion.

Justin's father Don was a long-haul trucker, disappearing for weeks on end, crisscrossing the country chasing loads. He specialized in hauling heavy machinery; tractors and backhoes, sometimes even military equipment that tore through transmissions and caved pavement on steamy days.

Tell you what boy," he'd say to Justin, poking the air with a bottle of Bud to punctuate every word, "there's no stopping my rig. If you're in my way, prepare to be road kill. A pussy-ass Toyota is a Jap speed bump to my Mack." Don loved all things large; his semi adorned with mud flaps featuring chrome outlines of women with colossal breasts, his Ford pickup jacked on special hydraulics to accommodate monster tires, even the coffee mug that perched on his dashboard could hold forty-eight ounces. His hairy, once-athletic body, nourished by a steady stream of foamy hops and chemically-enhanced baked goods, had ballooned to wooly mammoth proportions. Long black hair pulled back in an oily ponytail, Don's style sense favoured offensive tee-shirts and leather vests; a massive wallet tethered to his belt loop with a chunk of chain. Justin thought his dad looked like an evil biker dude from a 1980's Steven Seagal movie.

He was also a man of unusual opinions, usually hatched late at night on desolate highways while listening to twangy ultra-right-wingers and radio infomercials. Ringo, his favourite Beatle. Hilary Clinton a Soviet spy. The government placed drugs in the meat supply in some kind of mass mind control experiment. Obama and Jay Z had built a secret "coloured army" to invade conservative states. He refused to own anything with an Apple logo, it being well-known Steve Jobs was an alien.

Don also claimed he'd trained to be a Navy Seal, though he'd never been in the military. He told Justin he'd worked as a bounty hunter while still in his teens, though Justin's grandmother clarified he'd spent his summers detailing autos at Hankey Brother's Used Cars. Once when Don was drinking beer on the deck with his pretend friends, Justin overheard him tell a story about the time he'd had sex with the skinny star of the old TV show *Cheers* in the sleeper compartment in his truck. In Don's world, Shelly Long had a kinky thing for hairy truck drivers, and would cruise truck stops on the 1-405 looking for hook-ups. He considered himself quite the lady's man, often implying, even around his wife, that the average woman found his overt masculinity overwhelming.

After years of fast backhands and beatings from his father, Justin had learned to duck and keep his mouth shut, and stay clear when he was *in one of those moods*, had imbibed on more than three beers, or was flying on the amphetamines he gobbled to stay awake while driving, Don's cruelty as unpredictable as a summer storm. A few weeks earlier when Justin had come home carrying a near-perfect report card, dreaming of some kind of attaboy from his parents, his father had instead chided him for being a "goddamn nerd" then closed the conversation with a sharp smack to the back of Justin's skull. "Smart only gets you so far," he yelled at his son. "Don't you go thinkin' your shit don't stink just because you got a few stupid A's. You want to be a success in life you're better off having balls over brains."

Justin feared the only one in the family more mentally deficient than his father was dear old mom, her face molded in a strange vacant smile when she watched her husband toss him around. Shy and birdlike, she was ill-equipped for parenting, with all her love and affection reserved for her husband, even though Don wasn't the least bit hesitant to slam her against a wall when he felt irritable. At night when she returned from her cashier's job at

Pep Boys she seemed surprised to see Justin, as if she'd forgotten she had a child.

Justin wondered how he fared so badly in the parental lottery. He loved reading and math, and breezed through his school work. He listened to Public Radio, read newspapers and magazines—and not the ones his mother favoured that featured Jennifer Anniston on the cover. Yellow-haired and slight in stature, he bore no resemblance to either of his folks. Sometimes he fantasized he'd been kidnapped as an infant, and his real parents, successful and educated, doctors or professors, would return to rescue him. But lately, his senior year just months away, he worried that they wouldn't find him soon enough. He yearned to escape and disappear inside a college library, but Don made it clear that higher education was not in his future. "College is bullshit" he'd announced more than once. "The government just wants to saddle you with a bunch of debt that you can't get rid of, so you're beholdin' to them for the rest of your life. Plus, they pump your head full of all kinds of socialist ideas in those places. Better off being your own boss like me." Justin shuddered at the thought of being anything like his father.

The night Don arrived home unexpectedly he made an announcement at dinner. "Boy, I came home early this week because I have a surprise for you." The hair around Don's mouth was caked with salad dressing, and it occurred to Justin his father had the dining etiquette of a wood chipper. "Tomorrow we're going hunting. Head to the Checkerboard with Ted. He's got an elk camp, and we're gonna spend the weekend getting you your first kill."

Don was an avid hunter, spending every autumn weekend tramping the woods. Justin didn't understand the appeal, and hoped it was something his father would choose not to share. "That's great Dad, but I wouldn't want to slow you guys down. I know how much you like elk hunting. If just you and Ted want to go I understand."

"For Christ's sake," Don said. "Most boys would do anything to go hunting with their old man. You sit around here with your nose in a book, never doing anything a normal kid does. Time to man-up and get some fresh air. We'll be on the road at

6:00 a.m. tomorrow."

The next day, pre-dawn, they loaded up mildewed camping equipment and several rifles into his dad's F150. Ted was standing outside his rusty double-wide when they pulled up, drinking steaming liquid out of a dented metal Reddi Electric mug, and wearing a child's stocking cap. Ratty and black with a *Hello Kitty* logo on the front, it looked like something he'd found in an alley outside a grade school. Ted had long ago abandoned his front lawn as a place for vegetation, and it was now a graveyard for rusting cars and appliances, an ancient washing machine propped sideways at the end of the driveway like a Maytag lawn ornament.

Justin had been surprised his father could attract a friend until he met Ted. This was a man that made Don look like a Nobel Laureate, content to assume the Ed Norton role in their *Honeymooner* relationship. He threw his gear into the back of the truck and climbed into the passenger seat, pushing Justin to the center. Luckily Ted was as small as his father was big—Justin always assuming the result of a meth-enriched diet—so it was not too uncomfortable.

Despite the fact that it was 6:30 in the morning, Don and Ted began drinking beer as soon as they hit the interstate, even forcing Justin to take a sip. "When I was your age I'd drink a six pack by myself, then I'd find me some good lookin' 15-year-old nooky," Don announced as Ted cackled. "Fact is, I wouldn't mind a little 15-year-old nooky this weekend," which made Ted roar as he and Don high-fived.

There was a foot of snow on the ground as they exited the highway at Big Timber and headed into the hills. Ted's uncle owned several hundred acres of timberland, and Ted had come up a week earlier to build a campsite. By the time they started unloading the truck, fresh snow was falling, and Justin could feel the temperature plummet.

"This is going to be a special weekend for you," Don announced, pulling a long rifle from a tattered canvas case. "Take a look. This gun has been in our family for four generations. Originally made to shoot buffalo. Old, probably built in the 1880s. A forty-five-seventy. Worth a ton of dough." He handed it to Justin.

It was different than any gun Justin had ever seen. The thick barrel was octagon-shaped, a foot longer than a normal rifle, with a maple stock worn white on the inside edge. A single shot, it had a wide iron hammer that had to be clicked into position to fire. "It's a family tradition that a boy's first kill is with the buffalo gun," Don continued. "Your granddad and I both did it. Now it's your turn. This weekend you become a man. Kicks like a motherfucker. But that's part of the fun. And I tell you what, anything you hit with this will be dead. If it can take down a buffalo it can take down anything."

Justin had no desire to shoot a gun, much less one that *kicks like a motherfucker*, but he knew better than to show fear in front of his father. His dad set a beer bottle on a stump fifty yards away, then picked up the rifle. He pulled a circular lever behind the trigger, splitting it at the tail of the barrel, and allowing him to insert a thick shell into the chamber. He had Justin brace one arm on the corner of the truck's tailgate to steady the firearm.

"Put that bottle in the sights, right in the V at the end of the barrel, get that stock lodged into your shoulder tight, take a breath, let it out slowly, and squeeze the trigger. And kablooey— you will blow the fucker apart."

Justin shuddered in anticipation of the rifle's kick. "Quit shaking like a little girl, and shoot the goddamn bottle," his father said with annoyance. He tried to relax, slowly exhaled as if blowing out a candle, and pulled the trigger.

There was crack that sounded like lightening hitting a tree, and Justin was propelled backwards into the snow, as the stock kicked up a couple inches, hitting him in the chin. It felt like he'd been slammed in the shoulder with a sledge hammer, and he could taste blood in his mouth.

"Ka-blooey." Ted was hopping around laughing.

Justin was on his back, and Don, laughing too, reached down to take the rifle. "Kablooey is right, but you ain't much of a shot. Missed that bottle by six inches. Still, had it been an elk you still would have blown him apart. Good job boy."

Justin was on his feet, rubbing his shoulder and face, feeling something warm and unfamiliar. His father had a strange look on his face, and it occurred to him that this was what pride looked like. They walked to the bottle. He'd hit low and to the left, ripping four inches of wood off the stump. His dad put an arm around him. "Don't worry. You'll get to shoot it again. Next time at something moving."

That was what Justin was afraid of.

Two hours later they were jammed into the truck, creeping five miles an hour along a line of cottonwoods that trailed a creek. "Well lookee' there," Don said smiling. Four whitetail deer were grazing near a bend in the stream. Exiting the truck quietly, Don and Ted pulled rifles from the gun rack. Don wrapped the leather sling of his Winchester around his left hand and pulled the gun to his shoulder, dropping down to prop one elbow on the hood of the truck, head settling into his scope. "Get ready for venison steaks," he whispered. Justin stared at the little family, praying his father wouldn't shoot straight. The crack ricocheted off canyon walls, and for a second it appeared he'd missed, as the animals jumped in alarm and bounded into the trees, but the fattest of the group, a female, took three steps and slumped to the ground. Justin had an urge to vomit as Ted cheered and again slapped palms with his dad. "Nice shot Annie Oakley."

The two men giggled happily as they walked towards the downed deer. The animal's eyes were wide open, still struggling, blood staining out a neck wound. Don nonchalantly chambered another shell, and fired a shot into the deer's skull from his hip. Justin stumbled back as the men continued towards the dead animal. He fought the urge to cry, realizing it would just redirect the savageness to him.

Don unsheathed a wide Bowie knife from his belt. He knelt by the deer, rolled it to its back, and plunged the knife high just below the rib cage. There was a whoosh of air escaping, the smell metallic and pungent. "Boy, this being your manhood weekend, you get another treat. It's a family tradition that on your first hunt you get to take a bite out of the heart of the first kill of the day. Something the Indians used to do to their young braves to toughen them up. Transfer all the energy of the animal to you." He carved into the body cavity as blood bubbled and soaked into the snow.

Justin stepped back as his stomach bottomed-out. "You want me to eat the deer's heart?"

Don looked up and smiled. "Not the whole thing. Just take a good-sized bite. It's good for you. Natural. Full of iron. A hell of a lot better than those burgers I know you and your mom eat when I'm out of town." He reached elbow-deep into the deer. There was the sucking sound of water draining from a sink, and he pulled out the heart.

"No." Justin stumbled backwards, but Ted grabbed him and pushed him towards the deer.

"C'mon Justin. This is your initiation to manhood." Don grabbed his son with one hand and shoved the bloody heart into his face with the other. "Take a bite. See what it tastes like to be a man." He continued to smash it against his face, trying to work it into his mouth, finally giving up, and pushing Justin back into the snow. When he opened his eyes Don and Ted were standing over him. "You look like a real redskin now," the two were convulsing with laughter. "Here, clean yourself up." Don threw him a filthy towel from the back of the truck. While they dressed the deer, Justin scrubbed his face and hands with snow until his skin was sandpapered clean, trying to exorcise the taste of blood from his mouth, and the animal's pleading eyes from his brain.

Driving back to camp Don and Ted were in high spirits. His father grilled venison steaks, served with Wonder Bread, beer, and Jack Daniels. Justin ate silently in a corner of the tent, hoping to be ignored, but with half the Jack downed the two finally turned their attention to him. "So Justin," Ted said, "you're about the age a kid gets his cherry popped. You done the big deed yet?"

Justin thought Ted oozed perviness, constantly finding a way to insert a sexual comment into almost every conversation; the kind of man that society should probably incarcerate just for the disturbing thoughts that rolled around his head, much less what he would do given the opportunity. "No, I don't have a girlfriend," Justin answered quietly.

"No girlfriend?" Ted's voice rose sarcastically. "That's no excuse. You don't need a girlfriend to get laid. I don't suppose the real reason is you prefer boys? Don," Ted turned his head, "your boy ain't some kind of rump ranger, is he?"

Justin watched his father flush red, and he wasn't sure whether Don's anger would be directed towards Ted or him. "Hell, I don't know what he is," he finally said angrily. "I started fucking when I was twelve, so he don't act like my blood. Sometimes I wonder if some limp-wristed UPS man that banged my wife, and this kid popped out," he said, pointing at his son.

Luckily the conversation turned to a more upbeat discussion of Don's sexual exploits, and Justin retreated to his sleeping bag, wishing he could somehow disappear, hoping he would wake up somewhere else. Anywhere else.

The next morning Don and Ted were hung-over, but strangely energetic. Justin assumed there was something about killing that made the men more alive. When they opened the tent flap a heavy mound of snow caved-in. It had continued to come down all night as the temperature fell. "Holy shit, it's a cold one," his father said as he came back from taking a leak.

Thirty minutes later they were back in the truck, crawling through the snow in low-gear. They inched several miles into a smaller canyon, and Justin began to worry they'd get stuck.

"Boy, you get a special treat today. We're going to drop you at the bottom of this canyon, and Ted and I will drive back up and hike through it. I'm positive there will be elk or a good sized deer in there, and you'll be in the cat bird seat when we drive them out. I'll put you in the perfect position to get your first kill." They stopped at the bottom of the ravine, and Don pulled the buffalo gun out of its case, walking Justin to the base of a big tree. There was a downed log six feet away. He loaded the rifle, and handed it to Justin.

"We're going back up, and then we'll walk right down the center of this canyon. Should take an hour or so. Be ready. Those elk will run in front of us, and they have to come right by you." Don motioned at the tail of the canyon. "Don't fuck this up, and don't make any noise. It'll be an easy shot. A short one. Use that log to steady the rifle. And remember what I told you. Get the elk right in the V, take a breath, breathe out easy, squeeze the trigger, and kablooey. Hopefully a big dead bull. And I won't even make you eat the heart on this one." Don raised a gloved finger to his face and mimicked pulling a trigger.

Justin settled in behind the log as they drove away. Initially he was pleased to be alone, but after twenty minutes started shivering. The snow was in full gale, and he got up to move around, keeping one eye on the ravine, the valley now a white blanket.

At the one hour mark he got into position, but didn't see any movement. The temperature continued to fall, and he felt an aching numbness in his hands and feet. At the hour-and-a-half mark his toes felt like stinging icicles about to drop off his feet, and it suddenly occurred to him they might not be coming. *Maybe they'd broken down. Or this is some kind of joke, another manhood test? Maybe they're back at camp drinking, or sitting in the warm cab of the truck laughing at the thought of him out here.*

Justin thought about what his father said the night before—that he might not be his son. *Perhaps he was serious.* On more than one occasion he'd complained about having Justin around. "Boy, you're just lucky your Mom and I are against abortion, cause we sure never planned on having a blood sucker like you around. You can't imagine how expensive it is to have a rug rat, even a pip-squeak like you," Don would complain. If he really didn't believe they were blood he might be anxious to get rid of him.

He considered his options. Walking back didn't make sense. It was at least ten miles, with this snow he could easily get lost and freeze anyway, and if they were coming back he didn't want to be somewhere they couldn't find him. He could build a fire, but realised he didn't have a match or lighter, and he wasn't sure he could find enough dry wood. He considered finding shelter to weather the storm. Perhaps he could build a snow fort and hunker down. He'd read a story about a mountain climber that saved himself that way, but that guy had a sleeping bag and supplies. For the next twenty minutes he tramped around the tree trying to stay warm.

At the two-hour mark he heard movement in the trees, the snap of breaking branches, then six massive forms emerged, brown and black rugs against a white backdrop. A family of elk, slowly moving through the brush, heads nudging-up to eat low-hanging foliage. Justin pushed down into the log and brought the gun up, scanning for the easiest target. There was a big bull, wide rack on display, bringing up the rear. Justin swung the barrel in the elk's direction, placing him in the V, when he saw more movement to the left. His father and Ted appeared like dark ghosts at the base of the canyon, oblivious to the herd right in front of them. The snowstorm had grown to near white-out conditions, and they probably didn't know they were near Justin's position or approaching the end of the ravine. Justin swung the rifle to ten o'clock, placing his father's form in the V. He suddenly realised what an easy shot it would be, much closer than the elk. Just another hunting accident. An inexperienced boy on his first hunting trip accidentally shoots his father during a blinding storm.

But of course it was a crazy idea, killing your own father. *If he was actually his father.* The thought of life without Don made him pause. *The house would be so peaceful. No more fear. No more bruises for Justin or his mom to hide. And next year when he graduated, there wouldn't be anyone to stop him from going to college, from living the life he was supposed to live. But it was nuts. He couldn't possibly……*

Justin swung the rifle back to the elk, and the bull seemed to sense the movement, blurting some kind of grunt to alert his family as they moved into deeper brush. For a second Justin considered taking the shot, even if he would miss, to cover himself with Don. But then he realised he could never shoot something so beautiful, a creature that was just doing all he could to protect himself and his family. And missing would just elicit his dad's wrath.

He rotated the rifle back towards Don, now even closer, placing him in the V, and remembering his instructions. *It would be so easy.* Take in a breath, let it out slowly, squeeze the trigger, and kablooey.

***

Flower Behind Her Ear

Andrew Stiggers

Born in Paris, France, in a British expatriate family, Andrew Stiggers has lived overseas since childhood. He studied English Language and Literature at the University of Reading in the UK. He was a finalist for the Tasmanian Writers' Prize 2015, shortlisted for the Asia New Zealand Foundation Short Story 2014 competition and the Atlantis Short Story 2014 Contest, and a semi-finalist in the New Millennium Writings Fiction Award 39. He was also selected for the New Zealand Society of Authors Mentorship Programme 2015. He currently lives with his wife, son and two daughters in Auckland, New Zealand. More details on the author can be found at www.andrewstiggers.com.

Flower Behind Her Ear has a rather unique setting, both in terms of the plot and the locale. Judge Brett Alan Sanders says of this soulfully painted piece, "the passionate evocation of the island itself stands out."

From where he sat on the golden beach, the tropical island could be on the very edge of the earth. For there was nothing out there beyond the outlying reef except the wide expanse of the calm blue ocean and the distant horizon where a few white clouds in the sky met the sea.

He could hear wave after wave crashing up against the reef and washing over it, before dissipating into the lagoon full of brightly coloured fish that swam dreamily about the coral. The water looked so refreshingly pure and clean that he felt he could plunge straight in and drink it up.

And a cooling breeze blew through the branches of the coconut trees as he turned to gaze at the sun.

-

"More coffee, Hugo?"

"No, thank you."

"Some cake?" his sister tempted. The Black Forest chocolate gateau was their mother's recipe.

"No."

She glanced at him in disappointment before putting on a smile for the woman sitting with them in the wood-panelled drawing room. "Well, this is nice."

The other woman smiled back. "Yes, rather."

Centuries-old family portraits looked down on them from the surrounding walls.

Hugo slowly stirred the remnants of his cold coffee. Like swirls and ripples in the lagoon. He didn't want to make eye contact with his sister, knowing she would undoubtedly give him that stare again. She had been trying her best, she'd told him. *You can't lock yourself away. You have to meet people. Women. You have to find yourself a wife, Hugo - it's your duty as the last male heir of the von Glan estate.*

The visitor plucked up the courage to talk to Hugo again. "So I hear you were a captain in the army during the war?"

He stopped stirring his coffee. "Yes."

Like millions of others, he was a man forever changed by the true horror of the Great War, the senseless death and destruction. The look on their faces. He remembered the faces of his men, their bodies sprawled around him – so still… void of life.

Hugo couldn't stand being in the room any longer. "Please excuse me."

When he had left, his sister smiled apologetically to the other woman. "I'm sorry about that. He doesn't like to talk about the war… I'm sure he'll be back soon."

"Of course, how silly of me. I didn't think. Yes, it was a terrible time. I lost my brother."

The uncomfortable silence returned, and the visitor looked desperately around the room, trying to find something - anything - to talk about. She glanced over at a large, dark-oak bookcase through the open doorway. "You certainly have a lot of books."

"The library, yes, it's quite a collection. Our father was an avid reader. Come, let me show you."

As she followed Hugo's sister into the adjoining room, the woman noticed there were more family portraits on one of the walls.

The sister told her, "This is where Hugo spends most of his time."

The visitor went over to the bookcase and picked up a worn-out book that was lying on one of the shelves. Her face lit up as she started to flick through the pages. It was a sketchbook full of drawings - jungle scenes, beaches with palm trees, a church, strange looking birds, and men and women wearing wreaths and grass skirts.

She stopped at a particularly erotic drawing of a Polynesian woman, her breasts barely hidden by a flower garland. "My word!

116

These pictures remind me of those scandalous Gauguin paintings." Just saying the word scandalous excited her.

"Hugo drew them when he lived in Samoa."

"Samoa? Oh, how exotic."

-

The Samoan flycatcher bird was perched on a branch above him and singing out to the world.

"*Tulouna*. Greetings. Greetings to you, Hugo von Glan of the Kingdom of Württemberg, and subject to Kaiser Wilhelm II of Germany."

It was as if the spirit of one of the great Samoan orators of the past was performing a formal greeting to the guest of honour.

"*Talofa lava*. Welcome. Welcome to our tropical island paradise in the South Pacific, welcome to the Protectorate of German Samoa, and imperial playground in the sun for the empires of Great Britain and Germany and for the United States of America."

Having taken a break from supervising the Chinese coolies in the cocoa plantation, Hugo was sitting against the side of the palm tree in his white suit and white pith helmet, sketching the lush valley that rolled down from the forest-covered mountains towards the sea.

He imagined his sister back home enjoying some fine German chocolate made using cocoa beans from the plantation. She couldn't understand why he'd chosen to go to Samoa and had been unhappy to see him go. It was an urge to go on an adventure and see the world - to see something different – he'd told her.

This was certainly different. He looked up from his sketchbook and spotted a copper-striped, blue-tailed lizard running down the tangled woody vine that was growing around his palm tree.

Hugo started to outline the Catholic church in the distance, with its colourful stained-glass windows and whitewashed walls. He remembered the first time he had entered the church, the cool air inside a comfort on his red, hot face. How strange it was to see the congregation of native men and women dressed all in white, and then the surprise of hearing their beautiful voices when they sang.

That was also the first time he saw her.

Even though all the brown faces - men and women alike - looked the same to him, he still noticed her straightaway. There was something different about her. As he caught her eye she shyly turned her head away.

From that moment he'd known he wanted to be with her.

-

Up in his bedroom, Hugo stood at the open window, staring out at the dark pine forest that blanketed the landscape, and breathed in the cold air. The entire region was landlocked - there was no sea for thousands of kilometres all around.

He missed the smell of the salty sea air. In fact, he missed a lot of things and had found it difficult to readjust to living back in Germany. The red geraniums and pansies in the window box reminded him of the colourful tropical flowers in Samoa.

"Hugo, there you are." His sister had come looking for him. "How many times have I told you? You cannot hide yourself away."

The snow and winter would be coming soon, and he wasn't looking forward it.

"Please come back downstairs. You have to make an effort."

-

The villagers, together with their guests, were all seated cross-legged on woven mats in the large, open thatched fale. Hugo sat alongside the old plantation owner and their fellow Germans, feeling relaxed and happy and also slightly drunk.

The speeches in honour of the Governor had finished earlier that evening, and the parties were now performing the kava-drinking ceremony.

"Remember, you have to drink it slowly," warned the plantation owner.

The kava tasted bitter and sharp, his mouth becoming numb.

Hugo waited and watched as the kava cup continued to be replenished and passed from dignitary to dignitary, and then from villager to villager.

At last, it was her turn. The girl from the church was sitting with her family at the opposite end of the hut, and like the others she was wearing a flowing costume decorated with flowers. A frangipani flower was tucked behind her ear, delicate white petals with a deep golden-yellow centre.

He had been told how unmarried Polynesian women wore a flower behind the right ear to signal they were single, while those with a flower behind the left ear were married or attached. It reminded him of the Bollenhut pompom hats worn by women in some Black Forest villages back home - red for unmarried girls and black for married ones.

She drank slowly, her lips on the edge of the cup, her flower behind her right ear.

It was time for the singing and dancing. From where Hugo sat with his compatriots, he looked outside to where a group of male dancers were taking their positions on the village square. He pulled out his sketchbook and started to draw them, using the light from the nearby torches, admiring their chiselled chests and tattooed buttocks and thighs. He became mesmerised by the circles of fire as the men danced, twirling their fire sticks, frenzied by the beat of the wooden drums.

It was then the turn of the women. The girl was there among them. They danced with a gentle movement of their bodies in time to the music, their arms outstretched. He was still feeling the effects of the kava as he watched, her long legs partially hidden by the grass skirt, her arms seemingly beckoning to him. He forgot about the pencil in his hand, the half-completed sketch.

When the women had finished dancing, the girl left the others and headed away from the village square and behind one of the other fales.

He got up and followed her, guided by several lit torches along the path. She was weaving her way between bushes full of wild hibiscus and ginger when he caught up with her. Moonlight shone on her face.

Hugo smiled at her. "Talofa."

"Talofa."

He pointed to himself and spoke slowly. "I am Hugo."

She giggled. "And my name is Silefaga."

"You speak German?"

"Yes, my uncle taught me. He is an interpreter."

"I see. You danced well tonight."

"Thank you."

"I... I have seen you before at church."

"Yes, I know."

"Would you like to go for a walk on the beach?"

"No, I must go. My family are waiting for me."

"Yes, of course. Silefaga?"

"Yes?"

"See you on Sunday."

"Yes." She started to leave, then stopped. "We can go for a walk after church."

He watched as she continued on to a fale.

Looking down, he noticed something on the ground. It was Silefaga's frangipani flower.

He picked it up and smelled its scent - her scent - and holding it in his hand he headed over to the nearby beach where the waves called out to him.

-

"No, you mustn't touch that."

Having reluctantly followed his sister into the library, Hugo grabbed the sketchbook out of the visitor's hands. "It's ... it's delicate." He held on tightly to the book.

"Please, Herr von Glan, you must tell me about Samoa. It looks fascinating from your drawings."

"Well…"

His sister looked at him in encouragement.

Hugo reluctantly opened the sketchbook at the first page, where he'd drawn a variety of marine life - turtles and tropical fish.

"What is this?" The woman pointed.

"A shark's fin."

As they looked at other pages together, Hugo remembered more and more things about Samoa and described them to her, a long-lost passion returning to his voice. The countless sandy beaches, the heat of the sun, drinking a cool, refreshing sugarcane drink, and exploring up in the mountains where the humid rainforest hid countless waterfalls.

He talked about the good things the Germans had done - building schools, roads, hospitals. They had even trained local nurses. He talked about the chiefs and the old tribes and —

"So there used to be head-hunters?"

"Yes, but some time ago."

"Oh, I see." She sounded disappointed.

He decided to show her his drawing of a warrior to get her excited again, and recalled a rebellion by some of the natives who formed war parties armed with guns supplied by the Americans. He chose not to mention how a German warship bombarded one of the rebel villages and smashed its fort to smithereens. He also didn't mention the fact that when he got trapped in another village

Silefaga had protected him from the rebels. There was a beautiful fierceness in her eyes at the time, he remembered.

Hugo talked about the Samoans' love of music and described male dancers performing a slapping dance, full of energy and fun. He started to make some of the moves himself, to great hilarity.

"Even more fun to watch than a Bavarian slap-knee dance," the woman remarked.

His sister felt hopeful. *He's smiling.* This was the first time since the war that she'd seen him talk at length with someone.

Even the portraits on the wall seemed approving.

Hugo recalled the impressive sight of the double war canoes filled with hundreds of men rowing across the harbour, and the time when two prisoners managed to escape from the native Samoan policemen and flee into the bush. He also showed the woman the German governor sitting proudly in his horse and cart, the German eagle emblazoned on its side. It was funnier to look at in real life, he added.

He talked about Fa'a Samoa, their traditional way of life, and how the community would do activities together like one big family.

"Family is important to us. It is part of who we are," Silefaga had once told him.

He remembered all her family members sitting and talking in their fale, protected from the rays of the sun. Children climbing up the mango trees. Children jumping off the end of the wharf into the cool water. Children playing, smiling, laughing, happy.

He never once had to mention Silefaga. There was no need - no drawing of her existed.

-

It was another beautiful day in paradise and Hugo was looking forward to their trip together to the other main island.

Although he had managed to convince the governor to let him borrow the motorboat, Silefaga was hesitant to board, and tried to insist they use one of the canoes, but no, he wanted to show off. German ingenuity, he said.

The sound of the motor starting up disconcerted her and when Hugo laughed she gave him a stern look.

Parts of a steamer that had struck the reef were still visible from the harbour as they set off. They headed down the coastline and saw other damage a recent cyclone had caused. Her village was lucky compared to some of these others with their ripped apart fales amongst a few surviving trees. Paradise was not always so beautiful but – he looked across the boat to Silefaga – she was.

A fine spray of water on his face cooled him down as they crossed the strait in the balmy midday sun.

Nearing the other island, Hugo saw a mountain further inland that dominated the landscape.

They beached the boat at an isolated spot and he took out a hamper while she laid a woven mat on the sand. Like a lunchtime picnic in the manicured gardens of a baroque Schloss, he thought.

"Hugo, draw me."

He eagerly took out his sketchbook. He had been wanting to draw her for some time.

As Silefaga struck a pose the earth around them shook, and there was the tremendous sound of a large explosion from the mountain in the distance.

He dropped the sketchbook and reached over to hold her in his arms.

"Look, Hugo, the volcano's erupting again."

Smoke appeared from on top of the mountain.

He could feel her shivering body, breathe in the perfume of scented oil on her body. She smelled so intoxicating. Her mouth was close to his.

Don't worry, I will always be here for you, he thought.

Hugo saw that her face was very much alive, excited by the sense of danger. He felt it too. Nothing on this earth was going to stop him being with her in this moment. "I love you, Silefaga."

He kissed her sultry lips, just as a pocket of steam suddenly rose up, hissing, behind them.

"We'd better leave," he said reluctantly.

"Yes, hurry." Silefaga looked in awe at the mountain as ash started to fall down on them.

Hugo picked up the sketchbook and hamper, she grabbed the mat and they ran to the motorboat and sped back to the safety of their home island.

"You must leave, Hugo. The British will be coming soon."

News of the declaration of war had been received by the radio station and had spread fast across the islands. Germans nervously guarded the government offices, whispering to each other. *Did you hear? A fleet is nearby - it will only be a matter of days before they are here.*

A day later and the fleet arrived.

Who is it? Is it our fleet? No, it's New Zealand. They're asking for our surrender.

One imperial flag was lowered and another raised over the central colonial offices in the capital.

"Hugo, I was right. It's not safe for you now. You must leave."

"No, Silefaga, I will stay. I must see you tonight."

The village was deserted when he arrived. Everyone had left to attend an emergency meeting between the local villages to discuss recent events.

He had made up his mind to propose to her, to stay in Samoa - to be with her no matter what. Be with her family. The children. *This is my home now.* He looked at the fales. He could live here, or she could live with him at the plantation. He could buy the plantation from the owner - he had the money.

"I have something to tell you, Silefaga, but first, please let me draw you."

This time it was going to happen.

Inside the small fale near the beach she pulled down all the coconut leaf blinds. He had never seen her naked. She was always so modestly presented compared to some of her bare-breasted friends.

As she started to tantalisingly undress in front of him, Hugo took out his pencil and sketchbook and drew the outline of her beautiful, elf-like body, her tender hips, her —

He stopped.

And had to blink in disbelief as he looked between her legs.

His pencil dropped to the floor. "What... what are you?"

"I am *fafa... fa'afafine.*"

"But you are a man."

"No, I'm fafa. Hugo, it's okay."

Stunned, he felt his world fall apart all around him. "You're not a woman."

Embarrassed, she picked up her dress and covered herself. "No, I am fafa. It's me. Silefaga. Don't you love me?"

Fa'afafine... a boy brought up as a girl. How could he have ignored such an intrinsic part of Samoan culture? But... but she was so feminine, so *real...* she had to be a woman. She *needed* to be a woman, not something so... unnatural.

"I... can't. I can't love you - this isn't right."

"But it's still me, Hugo."

He walked out of the fale in a daze, brushing aside one of the blinds, and headed for the beach. *Don't look back.*

She was a man.

The shock was more devastating than the countless ones he'd feel in later years when thousands of shells rained down on him in the trenches.

Confused, ashamed, he kept walking briskly down the beach. He had to get away from this place.

Escape was a retreating German warship, taking him back to Europe and civilisation - and war.

Losing himself in the deafening madness and brutality, a senseless time when right and wrong didn't matter any more. Releasing his anger through the slaughter of men. Burying his emotions in the mud deep down in the trenches, away from the sky and the stars.

Never drawing again.

—

The afternoon was over and his sister, full of hope, saw the woman to the front door.

The visitor paused on the step. "You must come round to my house for coffee next week with your brother."

"Yes, that would be wonderful."

Left in the library by himself, Hugo stared at the sketchbook in his hand. From one of the pages he pulled out an envelope that had an overprinted German Samoa stamp postmarked 1919. The letter inside was from the plantation owner and described life on the island during the New Zealand occupation. Hugo reread the paragraph about another, much larger eruption of the neighbouring island's volcano, and the resulting tidal wave that had swept along the coastline of Silefaga's island, causing terrible destruction.

Obliterating her entire village.

He returned the letter back inside the sketchbook before carefully opening the last page and delicately lifting out an old pressed flower. The scent had long gone but its white and yellow colours were still vibrant. He placed the sketchbook in a drawer containing his old army revolver, then sank into the chair behind his desk, looking at the faded flower in his hand and thinking of what could have been.

Waves. The sound of the waves.

The portraits on the wall, the bookcase, the dark room started to disappear in front of him.

He looked down at his feet; his shoes were gone, and he pressed his toes into the warm sand.

He could smell the salty sea air. Up above, a flycatcher bird called out to him.

In front of him stretched the clear, still lagoon.

A breeze blew through the coconut trees, carrying a hint of scented oil, the fragrance of her skin.

Home at last.

-

His sister heard a loud bang, and came rushing back to the library. *No, God, please no.*

-

He sat on the golden beach, near the fale with the blinds down, and gazed forever at the setting sun, together with the woman wearing a flower behind her left ear.

***

Something Else Happened

Kristen Falso-Capaldi

Kristen Falso-Capaldi is the 2015 winner of the Victoria Hudson Emerging Writer Prize, and her story "The Absence of Cows" recently won first place in *See the Elephant* magazine's New Voices Contest. Her fiction has also appeared in *Underground Voices* magazine, in *FlashDogs : An Anthology* and on *The Other Stories* podcast. Her co-written screenplay *Teachers: The Movie* was an official selection for the 2014 Houston Comedy Film Festival. She is currently working on a novel. Kristen lives in Rhode Island, USA.

In *Something Else Happened*, Kristen explores loss, memories and pain through a gripping, and often intriguing first person narrative. Judge Brett Alan Sanders' experience with the story reads thus "Grabs you from the start and doesn't let go. A moving portrayal of mental illness and the way past memories sometimes continue to haunt."

A guy named Mongo lived just up the street, across from us in the little bungalow with the peeling door. He came up to me once on the way home from fifth grade and punched me in the throat. I doubled over coughing, and he gave me a head-butt. Then he shouted, in front of the neighborhood, "Your father is a drunk." He punched and kicked till I was a bloody mess, and my father, the drunk, pulled up in his old sedan with the tan roof, picked me up off the pavement by the back of my collar, and tossed me like an old shirt into our house.

Mongo was a short guy with bad posture whose whole body would quiver when he laughed, his eyes narrowing to slits and his voice cigarette-hoarse, even when we were kids. Those eyes never landed on you for long, as if he couldn't spare the time it took to focus on you. And he never talked; he shouted.

"Your father is a drunk," he'd yelled. So was his, and everyone knew it. Maybe Mongo was exorcising his demons. But smashing my head into the asphalt didn't change him. And it didn't change me, though I gulped up his blows with the greediness of a drunk.

The last I heard, he was in the Adult Correctional Facility, in maximum. A week after high school was over, Mongo and two other thugs from the neighborhood had beaten and raped a prostitute. They did something else. They cut her tongue out.

I've started thinking about Mongo and the old neighborhood again. I turned forty today, and every day for the last two weeks I've been walking down this street. Today, I live with my wife, my kids, a dog and a cat in one of those neighborhoods I used to wonder about, looking through the back window of my father's sedan. Our house is big, our yard is big and our big SUV will grow bigger with the next trade-in, when our three children and the dog and all their paraphernalia can no longer fit for the rides to soccer and baseball and dance classes. Sometimes, I'm not sure how any of it happened. How I got *there*, I mean. It seems, sometimes, like I am still *here*.

Growing up, I saw my future as an endless row of identical bungalows and drunk fathers. But something else happened. I applied to college because my high school girlfriend, an honor student whose face is just a blotch of cream and pink in my mind's eye, was going to Brown. I got into the state school, and we lost touch in a matter of weeks. But I was at college, so I kept going. My father died while I was away during sophomore year. My mother went into the nursing home five years later. Dementia. I started working at the insurance company right out of school, and I kept going. Now I've got a high level position no one understands, and I wear a tie and take trips to Disney World every year. Every morning I shower, shave, and watch out for objects in the back-up camera of my SUV as I leave the house. Sometimes, I think of it as a ride on a conveyor belt, and most of the time I stare straight ahead. But at other times, like today and these past two weeks, I need to turn around and look backwards.

People called me Babe back then. The adults in the neighborhood started calling me Babe instead of Ronnie because I played on the local church baseball team. I was good, I guess; though I don't think our team was very good. The kids called me Babe for a while too, but it was mostly the adults whose minds didn't wipe clean quite as quickly as kids.

I was Babe till the day I left. Ronnie to the other kids, mostly. I've been Ron for longer than anything else.

Forty. It blindsided me. I was moving along on my conveyor belt, and last week my wife asked me what I wanted to do for my birthday. The kids started yelling out the names of their favourite chain restaurants, and she kept saying, "It's Dad's decision. Let Dad choose." I looked around at them and I thought, "Who is Dad?" I felt as if someone had shot me full of Novocain, the numbness spreading down my arms and legs, across my forehead, reaching deep into my chest cavity. I had to leave the room. I stood in the bathroom and cried with the exhaust fan and water running, even though I made no sound. When I came out, they were still talking about restaurants, their voices loud, as if no time had passed since I left the table.

I'm supposed to be at a birthday lunch right now. The people in my department were taking me out to a steakhouse near the airport. I was on my way there when, I don't know how, I ended up on my old street instead. It's been the same every day. I park all the way down the opposite end, and I follow the route I used to take home from elementary school. It was the route I was taking the day Mongo ambushed me in the road between our houses. Every day, I half-expect the impact, the punch in the throat, the head-butt, followed by my back smacking against the pavement. I feel a vague surprise each time nothing happens and I am still alone, walking in silence. I look around at the houses I used to know so well. They've all seemed to shrink over the years. The houses in my current neighborhood could swallow these, and nobody would notice. But these houses hold something stored up in the spaces between the walls where the joists and the plates and the studs meet to form a structure. The one I lived in holds a moment that I revisit often.

It happened a few weeks before I started dating the cream-coloured girl. It was a long drawn out February school vacation in the middle of the longest winter I remember, one of those years where it just seemed to snow and snow. I tried to kill myself. No one was home, and I tied a phone cord around a beam in the basement and wrapped it around my neck. But when it came down to it, I couldn't do it. I stood there panicking, then I stood there shaking for a long time. I finally reached up and loosened the cord and pulled it back over my head. I coiled it up carefully, then stashed it on top of a beam way in the back of the basement. I promised myself I'd try again, and I wanted to. But something else happened. A month later, with the cream-coloured girl, Sheila, at my side, I applied for college. Then the conveyor belt life began. I wasn't Babe or Ronnie. Ron was on a trajectory, and every day has been movement in increments, but the truth is, sometimes I feel like none of it happened.

Maybe I died that day.

But the children holler *Dad!* at me when I'm daydreaming at the dinner table or falling asleep in front of the TV. They ask for handouts, deposits into their accounts of endless needs. My wife makes love to me, and each time I climax I think she takes a piece of who I am and stores it somewhere I'll never see. Sometimes she talks about one more child. There is so much space in this house, always the space that needs to be filled. Even with two adults, three children and a dog and a cat, there is endless room. I nod at her suggestion and stare straight ahead.

I walk by the places where things happened. A boy, Johnny's, tenth birthday party, the tree where that girl, Maddie, crashed her bike and lost a tooth, the house that everyone avoided on Halloween. An emaciated dog is tied up in the back yard of one house. It lifts its head, makes one futile bark, then returns to the act of being invisible. It almost looks like one of the mangy coyotes that creep into our backyard on summer nights. My wife tells the children over and over again that they have to look out for our cat and make sure she's back in the house at night. They answer her with distance in their eyes. Someday that cat will be eaten. I won't be able to stop it from happening.

My cell phone vibrates. "Ron, are we at the wrong place?" A text from Steve, my assistant manager.

"No. I am," I answer.

His return text is a series of question marks. I turn off my phone. Mongo's house looms up ahead. My tormentor for all those years lived in a lemon yellow bungalow with his cruel father and indecipherable mother, a four-foot-tall wisp of a woman who wore a stern expression and a tattered housecoat. His mother didn't talk to us kids. The only use for her voice, it seemed, was to shout at Mongo, or shout *for* Mongo. From inside the tiny house, the roar of Mongo's father. Our house sat on the other side of the street, symmetrical to Mongo's; a small gray bungalow with a red door. Our windows faced theirs, our door their door. I used to stay up late and watch Mongo's father from the upstairs window. He was always stumbling in drunk. Once he drove his car onto the front lawn and almost hit the house. I spent a lot of nights in that window, when I could've just turned my eyes inward to see my own father.

In a few minutes, I will stand in the middle of the road between our houses and remember Mongo's fist crossing through the coolness of the air. Of all the times Mongo tormented me, that was the only time he hit me. I had anticipated it for so long. And even as my nose gushed red onto my dark brown t-shirt, I mourned the loss of the fear. *Hit me again*, I would stare at him after that, but he wouldn't do it.

So my face healed, and my head stopped ringing. I sat in my classroom in fifth grade, sixth grade, rode the bus to junior high, went to high school, tried to kill myself, then met a girl named Sheila who led me to a guidance counselor who helped me fill out papers, then I sat in college, middle of the row. No one ever beat me up again. I didn't try to make friends or find a girl, but I got both. In college, I was the quiet guy who everyone liked. They called me the secret weapon; the guy at the bars or campus parties who did little but got all the female attention. I took girls back to my room and slept with them. Most of them got bored when they realised there was little behind my quiet but quiet. My wife was the one who didn't get bored. She talked enough for both of us.

I reach my old house and I stop, facing the peeling gray paint and overgrown lawn. It's empty. I stand in the middle of the street, looking straight through the front window. There are no curtains there. In the distance, I see nothing but the far wall.

"Hello," a voice behind me. I turn to face Mongo's mother. Smaller still and more shriveled. "Well, hello, Babe!"

Her face stretches into a toothless smile.

"Babe! You're handsome as ever!"

"Hi," I say.

"What are you doing here?"

"I turned forty."

She nods as if this explanation suffices. She glances at my old house, then back toward her own. I suppose she looks sad.

"I was just thinking about you."

"You weren't. You couldn't be."

"About you and Lenny, and Nick, those twins that lived down that way." She points. I don't remember any of the people she's talking about, then it hits me that Mongo's real name was Lenny, and it wasn't for Mongo she called all those years ago, but Lenny.

"Oh," I say.

"You're taller every time I see you." She looks up at me with amazement, like there isn't anyone quite this tall in this neighborhood. I stare back.

"Well, I've grown up."

"And I'm shrinking, Babe!" She chuckles, and her body quivers, her eyes become slits and her voice is cigarette-hoarse.

"How have you been?" I ask.

"Well, you know, Babe," she says. Her eyes are old and rheumy. She blinks at me. "I'm alone here now. But I find things to do."

Then, an awkward silence because we've run out of things to say.

"I was hoping to visit my old house, but it looks like it's empty."

"Oh, well, it's a terrible thing."

"What?"

"You know, Babe, " Her voice becomes gentle, like she's worried about how I will take what she's about to say. "Sometimes it's true."

"What's true?"

"You can't go home again."

I stare at her.

"You know. The boy who hung himself in that house." My skin grows cold. Then I feel it again, the numbness washing through my body.

"What? When? Years ago?"

She eyes me with concern. "No, Babe, *you* lived there years ago."

"Uh," I stumble. "I meant before me."

"Your grandparents lived there."

"Oh."

"I was talking about the teenage boy who killed himself two years ago. You knew."

"No! God! No I didn't know."

"I'm mistaken then, Babe. I was certain you knew."

I realise I'm shivering even though it's summer.

Then, before I can silence myself: "I'm really here, right?"

"Of course you're really here. You've grown into a fine looking man, Babe. A fine looking man."

"Sometimes I feel like I died that day."

"What day?"

"Am I still alive Mrs. Davis?"

"Of course you are, Babe. I'm looking right at you."

"Do you remember the time Mongo beat me up? It happened right where I'm standing."

Her eyes fill with tears.

"Lenny," she says is a small voice.

"Could I maybe go visit Mongo sometime?"

"Oh darling, Lenny isn't--"

Of course, I think. I shouldn't have said anything.

"When did he die?"

"He was still in prison."

"Oh." I imagine a knife sliding into flesh, men's heads bashed against prison walls and pain, tearing through his body as he choked blood.

"He got sick. Needles, you know. Prison doctors, you know."

"Oh."

She nods.

"I'm awfully sorry," I say.

"Well---"

She nods again and tells me she's had enough fresh air for the day.

"You take care of yourself, Babe," she says.

I resist the urge to ask her again if I'm alive, if she can see me, and I just wave as she walks into the house.

It doesn't take much to break into my old house. It's empty as I suspected, and the rooms seem both familiar and foreign to me. I wander through the small rooms, then up the narrow staircase to my old bedroom. I could see into Mongo's old bedroom if the shades weren't down.

I walk down into the basement, and with every creak in the aging wood, I feel the numbness draining from me, like water from a tub. I suck in a deep breath, then another and another, even though the air is so full of dust I can taste it.

The family who lived here must have left in a hurry. There are still clothes draped over the old washing machine, a few boxes scattered along the floor. I wander around in the dark using the little sunlight that filters in through the dirty windows to make my way. I stand under the beam. I close my eyes, remember the feel of the cord around my neck. The moment hadn't lasted long. And I stand remembering it. How I coiled up the cord so neatly, as if it mattered. And hiding it on top of a beam, another one, deep in the dark recesses of the basement. No one ever knew it was there. Afterwards, being afraid that someone would know just by looking at me. Telling myself that the next time I wouldn't be a baby about it. Then, meeting Sheila at the roller skating rink and making out with her near the snack-bar. Never telling anyone.

Despite what Mongo's mother said, it does seem possible that I died that day. That I didn't start shaking, that I never met Sheila or made out with her. That people knew because they found me. There was no college, no girls in the dorms, no job, no marriage, no kids, no SUV, no trips to Florida. That I was and still am a corpse in the ground somewhere. I start shaking again. The numbness spreads. I'm not sure what I want the truth to be.

There is, of course, the possibility that something else happened. I tried. I started shaking, then somebody found me just as I pulled the cord back over my head. My mother. My father. One of them came down into the basement and saw me trying, failing, shaking. My mother put her hand to her mouth and stifled a silent scream; my father grabbed me by the collar, pulling me back up the stairs into the light of day. They sent me away for awhile. I never met Sheila or made out with her. I never applied to college on a whim. I am someone else, living - maybe happily, perhaps not - somewhere else.

But of course I know. I know that when I walk back up the street, my SUV will be there, and when I turn on my cell phone, there will be texts from people who are trying to bring me back. That's where I can find the truth if I really want it. But the truth for me is down in this basement. That cord is still here. I know it.

I walk the length of the cellar, back to where the sunlight doesn't reach. It's impossible to see my way and I stumble around, barely picking up my feet as I feel for solid ground with every step. I find the beam, the one that ran the length of the back storage room. I reach up and feel around. My fingers come back covered in dust and cobwebs. Panicked, I run my hand along the length of the beam; a splinter pierces my skin, but I keep at it, back and forth with my fingers through the dust and mouse shit and dead bugs. But the phone cord isn't there.

I rush back up the basement stairs and through the house into the fresh air. I hold onto the porch railing and try to cough out the dust. I glance over at Mongo's house, and a curtain swings back into place.

I sprint back to my car and jump in, peeling away from the curb and speeding all the way to the steakhouse near the airport. When I get there, my employees are getting into their cars and heading back to work. I don't call out to them.

When I get home from work, my wife and children are already waiting to take me out to dinner. I try to resist, tell them that I am not feeling that great, but the children are not listening.

My wife squeezes my arm and stares at me till I turn to meet her concerned eyes. I let her lead me out to the car. All through dinner, I play along and wait for the table conversation to turn away from my birthday to my sons' baseball tryouts, my daughter's eighth birthday party, which is coming soon, my wife's yoga class. When it does, my mind drifts back to the basement, the cord, the empty beam. I press the place on my finger where the splinter is still imbedded in my skin. What happened to that cord? Did the young boy use it? Did I? I press harder on the splinter and stare straight ahead. I'm here, I tell myself. *You're here.*

When we return, my sons go upstairs to play video games, my daughter flips on the TV and my wife makes tea. She smiles at me, but in her eyes she holds a tiny speck of something. She wanders off to bed and I head downstairs to the basement. We finished our basement when our first son, Mitchell was born. My wife wanted the kids to have a place to spend time with their friends. I am the only one who uses the room, with its big screen TV and sectional sofa. I often find myself falling asleep down here, in the quiet with the TV on mute. This is what I do tonight, I lie on the sofa and flip through the channels before settling on an old movie, pressing mute and closing my eyes. But I don't fall asleep.

"You made it through 40. You're alive." I speak the words out loud, close my eyes, but sleep remains elusive. Where is that phone cord?

Without thinking, I get up and open the door to a small portion of the basement that isn't finished. It rumbles; the furnace is inside, the hot water heater, an oil tank and several crates, things that belonged to my wife from before this house, before the kids. There isn't much.

I walk around in the dark, running my hand along shelves or touching the tops of bins. My wife's boxes take up most of the space, and even hers don't add up to much. She's got some old high school and college yearbooks, a few photo albums, maybe some schoolwork from when she was a kid. There are four bins that belong to her. I don't have enough stuff to fill a bin, but there's a suitcase I'm looking for. It's old and weathered, and I know that when I open it, I'll find old photos that belonged to my father. They represent his younger days, when he was in the army, or just after when he came home. When he met my mother one night at the roller skating rink. There aren't any in here from when he was my father. In every photo, his eyes lock on the camera with the stare I thought I'd forgotten. He never really hit me. He didn't have to. His eyes did all the work for him. I wanted him to. I imagined the blows many times.

I sit on my wife's bins, thumbing through the loose photos, there are so many of them, but my mind doesn't stray from the cord. I rest my hands inside, gathering fistfuls of photos and try to think. Could the boy have found it? That must be the reason it wasn't there. Or something else happened. Someone else found it, years after me, but before him. I don't realise that my fists are squeezing the photos in the box, almost as if I am picking up handfuls of beach sand, until I hit something on the bottom of the suitcase. When I slide my hand under the photos, bent now from the weight of my palms, I grip something. I pull it out from the suitcase, spilling photos everywhere. Fifteen pairs of my father's eyes reproach me from the floor.

"Oh God! God!" I don't realise I'm yelling till the lights pop on in the stairwell and my wife is standing in front of me.

"Babe, what's wrong? Babe?"

"Why are you calling me that?"

"What's wrong?" She puts both palms on either side of my face, looks me straight in the eye.

"'Babe'! Nobody's called me Babe since that day."

"Calm down."

"I'm really dead, aren't I? I'm dead!"

"What--?" Her face hardens when she sees what I'm holding in my hand.

"That day in the basement, with this--it worked." I shake the coiled phone cord in front of her face.

"Oh God."

"Why did you call me 'Babe'?"

"It's just a word, I call you *babe* sometimes, or *honey, sweetie.* They're just words." By the time she finishes her sentence, her tone turns harsh, and her hands fall from my face and hang limp at her sides. She looks down at the phone cord, and I am about to tell her how I was lost on that day in February all those years ago, how I just wanted to feel something, and how I stashed the phone cord on a beam. But now it's here, as if it followed me. How I don't know if Ron is real, because Babe died and Ronnie is still out there. I hold the phone cord out at the end of my arm and stare at it, my eyes and mouth open wide.

She stares at me. Her eyes have gone cold. And when she speaks, her voice is hot. It burns my face.

"Where did you get that, Ron?"

"What do you mean?"

"Why are you doing this again?" Her voice trembles and her eyes grow colder still.

"It's the same one I tried to use-- back then."

"It's not. You've been walking down that street again, haven't you?"

I just look at her.

"You can't keep going to that house, Ron. You can't keep obsessing over that poor boy."

"I was that boy."

"No. You didn't die. He did."

"Maybe we both died."

"You're alive."

"Maybe something else happened. I'm alive, but I'm somewhere else. Not here."

"You're alive, Ron. And you're *here.* I should know. I am the one who always has to stop you. I am the one who keeps thinking it's over. Then you buy another one and it starts again. What happened this time?"

"I turned forty."

"Come on to bed," she says to me. Her sigh is heavy. I feel the weight of it. "We'll call Dr. Maxwell in the morning."

She leads me up the stairs, past my children who are all awake now and cowering from me.

"I'm ok," I say, as I let myself be led toward my bedroom. My sons and my daughter look toward the floor.

In bed, my wife gives me a Diazepam, and she assures me again that Dr. Maxwell will fix everything.

"I'm sorry," I say.

"I know."

"This is the last time. I promise."

"Good night, Ron," she says as she turns out the light.

"I know Babe is dead," I whisper into the darkness. "But what happened to Ronnie?"

My wife sighs and turns in bed so her back is to me. I turn to my side and drape one arm over her. A long time passes, but eventually, with another sigh, she takes my hand. I stare at her back, the way it becomes concave when she breathes. How you'd never notice it, because the movement is so minuscule; but I do. How she's not sleeping, just very still.

***

Long John of Babylon

Bruce Campbell

Bruce Campbell is a writer of short stories and novels from Portland, USA. He has recently been published by The Timberline Review, and one of his short stories was placed first in the 2015 Kay Snow Writing Contest. He also operates an urban farm and climbs mountains. In 1999, he led the first group of high school students along the Nez Percé National Historic Trail, a project documented in the publicly released film, Journey of Heart & Spirit. He plans to hike the American Discovery Trail from Delaware to California, where he hopes to unearth a new idea for his next novel.

Long John of Babylon is an engaging, surrealistic piece about childhood and motherhood, both dwarfed in the arms of destiny. Judge Anisha Bhaduri says "There is a place called desolation is our hearts. And there's sunshine called faith. Bruce Campbell tells us in tight sketches how faith can displace desolation, even dwarf it. And when it can't, life will. That's how masterful he is."

Long John's eyes crack open. It's late morning, but a dream still growls in his left ear. He clenches his jaw and hears a woman's voice:

She rises from the sea. Life is short.

Long John gasps for air, his heart jittery. Tears streak his cheeks and he tastes salt at the back of his throat. Putting on his horn-rimmed glasses, he slides naked from bed, crosses the concrete basement floor to the box refrigerator, and opens it. In a slough of greasy light, two cockroaches hump a stub of Italian salami. Long John closes the door, pads over to the washbasin, and clambers up the wobbly metal stepladder. In the cracked mirror, he sees his porcini brown eyes, elfish nose, and tight round mouth. He swats blanket lint from his black curls and pisses into the washbasin.

Climbing down the ladder, he puts on child-sized boxer shorts, red polyester slacks, a green flannel shirt, wool socks, and size six platform shoes with brass snaps. A beige nylon windbreaker and a tweed cab hat seal the deal. He scoops ocean sand from his coat pocket and lets it dribble between his fingers.

She rises from the sea. Life is short.

Slapping grains of sand off his hand, Long John exits his basement studio and climbs to the top of the outside stairs. Hugo, an oversized nine year-old foster child, blocks his path. Hugo often waits for him on the steps, like a Schnauzer keen to ambush a gopher.

Long John confronts a naked rump. Hugo's turned upside down turtle-style, short pants down to his ankles, his exposed rectum an exploded nectarine. He strikes a wood match on the steps and holds it close to his anus. A lizard tongue of yellow green light flares. Hugo's face swivels into view, his eyes bulging.

"Hah!" he cries. "Best one yet." He stands and pulls up his shorts.

"No school today?" Long John asks.

"No school."

"Why?"

"Hugo get mad, Mr. Mini-Man. He flushes all his pills down toilet. No pills, no school. Now Hugo stay home play with Mr. Mini-Man."

Long John tries to squeeze past Hugo, but the child seizes his arm clam-tight and stares down at him.

"Easy now."

"Need money, Long John. Need a million bucks."

"How about a quarter?"

"Hugo's new mom says you got pots of gold under a rainbow."

Using his free hand, Long John scoops sand from his windbreaker pocket and brings it close to Hugo's nose. "Here's your million."

Hugo sniffs the sand. "Don't smell like a million bucks."

"It's stardust, Hugo."

"Like candy?"

Long John points at the sky. "We come from the stars. We're all stuffed to the gills with stardust."

"Hugo says shit on the stars."

Long John returns the sand to his windbreaker and pulls a quarter from his pants pocket. "Here's two bits."

Hugo takes the quarter, releases his arm, and narrows his eyes. "We play rat and dog. You're the rat."

Long John gains the top of the stairs and edges away. "Later."

"You mad?"

"No."

"Everybody mad at Hugo."

"I'm not everybody."

"Hugo bust down your door."

"Ah, well . . ."

"Hugo cut tongues from your shoes and rip zippers from your pants. Come on, let's play rat and dog."

Long John tosses another quarter. It strikes Hugo's shoulder and bounces down the steps.

He sets a course for the bus stop, Hugo's barks and howls chasing him down the street. Long John recalls *Omega Acres*, the Catholic orphanage that's still a raw memory of his dog-chewed childhood. *Omega Acres*, a temporary home for him, and a permanent one for the Mastiff which had seized him like a soup bone, leaving a fossil record of teeth marks along Long John's belly and backbone.

The bus squeals to a stop, pneumatic doors hiss open, and Long John steps up into a stratosphere of human stench. The driver scoops petroleum jelly from a jar and fingers it into his nostrils. He rolls his eyes down to Long John.

"How low do you go, Monsieur Vincent van Gogh?"

"Got the nosebleeds again, Gus?"

Gus wipes his fingers on his trousers and grins, his teeth square and yellow. "My honker's on the rag. That time of the month, so don't get sideways with me."

"How about half fare today?"

"You half to be kidding, Long John."

"Too short for half off, eh?"

"Yeah, too short. Same thing my wife tells me."

The bus lurches forward, throwing Long John off balance. He grips the metal railing and grins up at Gus.

"Guess what?"

"Surprise me."

"Gonna try out for the Giants."

"The Giants don't need a shortstop." Gus chuckles at his joke.

"I'm a born baseballer—like Eddie Gaedel."

"Eddie who?"

"Eddie Gaedel. In 1951, he came to bat for the old St. Louis Browns. He was a midget. Wore number '1/8', and had an inch and a half strike zone. Eddie got walked four straight pitches. Publicity stunt, of course."

"Stunts for runts. Ha."

"Had a great career, Gus. At parties, he played midget-in-the-cake."

"You mean midget-in-the-shortcake."

Long John stumbles down the aisle and takes a seat next to an old woman with a freeze-dried complexion and yellow poodle curls protected by plastic wrap.

"Nice day," says Long John, his legs dangling over the seat edge.

The woman tilts toward him, licking her lips. "Nice day, you say? What you know about nice day, little monkey? In Estonia, nobody have fucking nice day."

Long John moves to another seat. The bus cuts a jigsaw route into the belly of the city. Gus pounds the bus horn, flips his middle finger at other drivers, spits out the window, and sings *Le nozze di Figaro*. Homeless people huddle against storefronts, sparrows and pigeons peck at a swatch of dried vomit, jackhammers bust up the street, and a woman with a purple shag plays hopscotch with young girls in school uniforms.

Getting off downtown, he wades into the swift crosscurrents of pedestrians, dodging kneecaps, knuckles, and hips, the air hot and sour. He hears a streetcar rumbling toward him, smells hot grease, sees a rooster tail of sparks, and catches the glassy smear of the passengers' faces.

A man stands on the curb across the street, his white high-top tennis shoes offset by hairy legs. He wears a sandwich board:

JESUS IS COMING! HOW ABOUT YOU? CALL SALLY'S MASSAGE PARLOR FOR HAPPY ENDING. The man steps off the curb, one leg poised above the tracks, and the streetcar strikes him. Long John hears the screech of steel. The man collapses beneath the streetcar. The sandwich board buckles and splinters. People scatter, colliding and gasping, sobbing and pointing.

Somebody jostles Long John, and bracing himself, he and sees a young woman towering over him. Twigs and leaves snarl her long brown hair, and on her white skirt, a dark red spot glowers at him like a disembodied eye, holding him in place. She says something to him, but he can't hear her.

"What?" Long John shouts.

"I found you," she says, her voice louder now, her green eyes spilling sunlight.

"You hurt?" Long John points at the woman's stained skirt.

She crouches, bringing her face even with his. "I must tell you a story."

"Please make it a short story."

"I'm sitting under a tree," she says, "in the park. A dead squirrel drops into my lap. It's covered in blood."

"City squirrels," says Long John, "die all the time."

"There was no dead squirrel," she says. "It was actually my dead baby."

"Oh. Sorry."

She clasps his hands and draws him toward her. "You're my dead baby, my child come back from your long sleep in the sea."

"Please let go of me," Long John says, "or I will bite you."

She tightens her grip and cups the back of his head with one hand and forces his face into her crusty green sweater, dislodging his hat, pushing his glasses sideways. "Your skin's so soft and sweet," she says. "Just like a little doll made from sandalwood and satin."

His face pressed into her breasts, Long John feels an erection stirring to life, and wrenches himself free. He rearranges his hat and glasses. "I'm strictly snips and snails and puppy dog tails. Sorry."

She brings her lips next to his ear. "Are you ready?"

"Ready for what, for chrissakes?"

She stands and tugs him through the crowd, his body skipping over the pavement like a bobber on a fish line.

"Let go of me!" Long John demands. "I'm not a stuffed animal!"

Recalling the unlucky sandwich board man, he imagines the amputated legs flopping on the hot tracks. Long John wants to borrow those legs and run away from the woman and her crazy talk about dead babies coming back to life and crawling from the ocean.

He yanks his hand free and bolts across the street, fighting against the bump and grind of the crowd. Glancing back over his shoulder, he sees the woman following, walking slowly, her palms up. The seaweed curl of her hair encloses her neck and shoulders. On her skirt, the bloody red eye ripples into view.

Long John flees inside a theater. The marquee reads FAMILY FUN CENTER. The carpeted lobby smells of ammonia and nicotine. The woman stands outside, gazing at him, and he feels the stab of her green eyes. She remains on the sidewalk, her upturned palms cupping sunlight.

A pit bull sleeps on the threadbare carpet near Long John, its slobber pooling up around its slack jaws. A theater employee, wearing yellow sunglasses and a red beret, leans over the ticket counter and stares down at Long John.

"Playing or paying?"

Long John hands the man a crumpled ten-dollar bill.

"Another sawbuck gets you a scratch'n'sniff card."

"I'm fine. What's showing?"

"A kiddie show," says the man. "One size fits all."

Long John enters the dark auditorium, gropes his way down the aisle, and sits close to the front. Placing a hand in his coat pocket, he squeezes sand. On the silent screen, he sees naked children. In slow motion, they bounce on a trampoline. Around him, Long John sees the hunched profiles of the other patrons. He hears groans and phlegmatic snuffling.

The camera zooms in on a girl's rigid thigh before lingering on the guitar string muscles of a boy's shoulders. A large red SCRATCH! throbs across the screen followed by SNIFF! Fingernails claw cardboard, nostrils whistle, the air a vaporous blanket of sweat, mildew, and fortified wine.

Long John visualizes Hugo on the trampoline, a flatulent toad bloated with the gas of the unloved. Thinking about Hugo makes him weary—and sad. He hangs his head, closes his eyes, and nods off.

She rises from the sea. Life is short.

He jerks awake, shivering, the dream voice drifting away. The screen's dark, the theater vacant and cold. He walks back into the lobby, but sees only the sleeping pit bull. He steps outside. Night has fallen. How has the time passed so quickly? An electric bus hisses past, a truck screeches, and Long John shivers.

The woman lingers on the curb, arms folded over breasts, strands of blue and red neon in her hair. He sees the bloody eye on her skirt, but in the street lamp, it's a purple-black blob. She steps forward, one hand extended, and smiles. She has two missing front teeth.

Darkness snakes into his bones, and he reaches into his pocket and scoops out some sand. He dribbles it between his fingers and sighs. Taking the woman's hand, he feels a brief jolt of electricity and almost pisses his pants.

They walk silently through the spectral gloom of street lamps. From behind a building's double-plated glass, mannequins leer at them. Long John hears the shuffle and thump of somebody else's footsteps. The amputated legs follow them. Magic is afoot. He's sure of it.

On the corner, a barefoot man plays a violin, the vibrato pitch of his instrument rising from the pavement. As they pass, he bows low, his shaggy gray beard brushing the sidewalk. The woman places two quarters at his feet and nods at him.

Next to a vacant lot, she releases Long John's hand, leans close, and caresses his face. "You belong to the sea," she whispers.

Long John gazes up at her chalky white face, her eyes divots of shadow.

"Life is short," he whispers.

Soon they come to a concrete seawall and Long John hears the rhythmic slosh and crash of surf. They descend a stairway and clamber across heaps of rotting seaweed, their footsteps weaving a path between darkness and moon-polished sand.

She stops, removes his glasses, and flings them away.

"I can't see!"

"Shhhh," she says. "Go to sleep."

She pulls him toward the surf, her superior size and strength overcoming his resistance. Saltwater floods his throat and blisters his eyes. He spins through a mosaic of darkness and light. Another wave hits, but the woman holds him fast. She guides him into deeper water, and she cradles him in her arms. In a slow, strangulated whisper, she sings:

The waters of Babylon

Oceans so deep

Soon you are gone

Gone to sleep

As if undressing a child, she peels off his clothes and unsnaps and plucks off his platform shoes. She sheds her own clothing. In the churning surf, he catches a ragged glimpse of her white skirt. Its wet red eye winks, spins, and disappears. The woman's arms encircle him, and then her legs, her hydra tight embrace pulling him into her breasts. Long John coughs and gasps, struggling for air. Death is a dog. It's always been a dog, and now the dog locks its teeth around his belly and backbone. Long John plays dead, but a voice growls into his ear.

Who are you?

Long John of Babylon.

Guess what happens next?

He knows what happens next, but he keeps his mouth shut. Perhaps he'll rise from the ocean, gasping for air like a newborn babe. Perhaps he'll swim to shore, find the amputated legs, and try them on for size. He'll be a new man, proud, tall, and strong. He'll be larger than life.

***

The Loudest Laugh of All

Siobhan O'Tierney

Siobhan O'Tierney is a maths teacher, keen on reading & walking but most intensely keen on all and any kind of gossip. She used to be fond of travelling but prefers armchair travel now, reading travel books from all eras, to all terrains. Her works have been published in various short story magazines and websites including Panurge, The New Writer, QWF, Northwords, DarkTales, and The Red Line, among others. She is also a regular scrabble player.

The Loudest laugh of All is a story about choices, and the inevitability of every choice and its consequence. "I thought the quality of the writing was high, with some gorgeous moments, and the characterisation strong", says Judge Clare Wallace about this story.

After all these years I realise – or am finally admitting to myself - I love Fraser.

But what's the use?

Harriet and I were placed together at a double desk on our first day at St Catherine's High School and after an hour she said to me: 'I can't believe how much you talk. Nobody has ever talked so much to me before.' I didn't believe her, until I met her parents. They were both dentists and she grew up in a detached house with a library and a garden we could get lost in. All that just made her a martyr to guilt about everything except board games. I lived two blocks away in a two-bedroomed flat with no garden. My mother was an auxiliary nurse and my father was dead. Once I asked my mother how he died: 'Coming home from the pub blind drunk, he went slam bang into a lamppost, collapsed and split his skull on the kerb. Like that!' She snapped her fingers like gunshot. 'Dead on the spot!'

It sounded like something in a cartoon and I laughed for a moment, then asked: 'But what was he like?'

'To be honest with you, Mary, t'was no loss. Not like when my father died. My father was a gentleman and a scholar. He had the wisdom of Solomon. He got nothing but the height of respect from all who knew him. There wasn't a better postman the length or breadth of Munster. There was nothing he wouldn't do for anyone, saint or sinner. He'd give you the shirt off his back. There wasn't a place he could go that he wasn't welcome as the flowers in May. Never forget you're Mick Tumulty's granddaughter. They came in their thousands to his funeral….

There was zero chance of me forgetting I was Mick Tumulty's granddaughter – my mother refused to change her surname when she married, and made it mine too. She never missed a chance to mention her father, and growing up in Ballyboreen.

My mother had eight siblings and innumerable aunts, uncles and cousins. Her childhood sounded hectic with poverty, tenacity and bitter feuds but it was her triumphs which she most loved to recall. Some of her stories made me ache from laughing, others made my heart hurt. A brother used to beat her black and blue: 'PJ couldn't stand how fearless I was. It drove him mad altogether so he always took his temper out on me.'

A sister was bitterly jealous: 'Peggy hated how I was Daddy's favourite. Of course I'm far more beautiful than her too so the bitch did everything in her power to thwart me.'

I couldn't bear how she'd suffered so much all her life with people turning against her from outright jealousy, and every night I finished my prayers with a vow to never fall out with my mother.

Every July we travelled by bus, ferry, and bus again, to Ballyboreen for a fortnight's holiday. My mother saved all year for it so I could never tell her how much I hated misunderstanding everyone's accent and visiting all the relatives whose names I could never match with faces. At night the only entertainment was playing cards and incomprehensible laughter, shouting and swearing. PJ always played so fiercely he seemed insane to me. I spent every day and night wishing myself back at home with my mother to myself.

Yet I think leaving Ballyboreen broke my mother's heart. Two years after moving to Glasgow she met my father at a dance and fell for him when she heard his grandfather hailed from Ballyboreen. 'That and his dimples. You got his dimples, Mary. Thanks be to God that's all you got from him. Little did I know then that Al Murphy was tight as a Turk and a drunkard to boot. Oh but he kept off the booze right up until the day he led me down the aisle and trapped me into marriage. God love me I was so innocent.'

The first time Harriet invited me to her house for dinner, the quietness there was like stumbling into a new galaxy and meeting a new species of humans. Her parents, her little brother, Harriet and I sat at a table longer and wider than our kitchen at home. The cloth covering the table was the whitest thing I'd ever seen. I couldn't believe how little Harriet's parents spoke and yet they didn't seem annoyed about anything and her mother smiled a lot. That might have been because her teeth were so good.

After we'd been eating in bizarre silence for some minutes, Harriet's mother asked me: 'Do you like school, Mary?'

I was still answering her as their house-keeper Betty was clearing away the desert dishes. Harriet said my impressions of all of our teachers were spot-on but it was her little brother Fraser who laughed most – a wonderfully chuckling laugh that made me feel so gifted I kept on exaggerating different teachers' voices (also, nobody interrupted me). Fraser had the loveliest brown eyes I'd ever seen and a full head of thick wavy black curls and seemed like a little prince in a fairy tale.

After dinner Harriet asked me: 'Do you like playing cards, Mary?'

My heart sank.

'Please play cards with us?' Fraser smiled so sweetly I felt my head nodding.

'We'll play pairs,' Harriet announced, deftly spreading the cards in perfect rows. In a flash she was transformed from the girl I knew at school who froze when spoken to, to playing as ruthlessly as my uncle PJ. Each time I picked mismatched cards she cried, 'Tough luck, Mary!' and laughed. But Fraser kept looking at me so sympathetically I longed to pick a pair just to cheer him up. In the end Harriet beat him by two pairs, while I failed to get any at all.

'Bad luck, Mary,' Fraser said sorrowfully, 'but you'll definitely win next time.'

I burst out laughing, it was so funny seeing a little boy trying so hard to cheer me up.

Primary school had been easy for me but the homework got much harder in St Catherine's. The only place where I could work at home was at the kitchen table and so, for the first time in my life, I started wishing my mother talked less. One night, when she started telling me yet again how she'd once out-witted the most notorious Garda ever to draw breath in Ireland I said: 'Tell me this later, Ma, I'm trying to do my homework.'

'Tell you later? Pardon me, Miss Too-busy-for her-own

mother! Fat lot of good those books will do you! My father left school at twelve and never needed any ol teachers' telling him what to learn! Father Clery once said he'd never met a better educated man than Mick Tumulty ......'

I understood my mother couldn't be in a room with someone without talking to them – unless she was sulking and made even more noise. So I started going to Harriet's house more often and we'd do our homework together. But my mother complained every time I went. One night I pleaded: 'But this maths homework is for tomorrow and I can't do it without Harriet's help.'

'Ooooh, "I can't do it without Harriet's help!" Why can't Lady Harriet come here for a change? Why are you always running to her like a lackey?'

My jaw fell – she hated anyone coming into our flat.

'Ha! Just as I thought! No reason her Ladyship won't come here only she's too high and mighty. Bet she wouldn't come for all the gold in China if you invited her.'

Two days later Harriet came home from school with me. My mother was so icily polite I couldn't wait for the visit to end. Soon as Harriet left that evening my mother snorted: 'Christ! How do you stand that one? The accent on her! And what about that nose! I've never seen a snootier nose in my entire life. As for how she looked me up and down!'

'Harriet didn't look you up and down. She's just shy,' I offered hopelessly.

'Shy my arse! Stuck up. That's all her problem is. Christ Almighty, Mary, you're a Tumulty! I cannot believe the granddaughter of Mick Tumulty is duped so easily by such rampant snobbery! I never reared you to turn out so treacherous and shallow! And I wouldn't mind but her ankles are so thick she has the legs of a fool.'

That was the first time I realised so starkly how randomly and irrationally my mother took against people, and also that trying to change her judgement was pointless.

After our homework, Harriet always wanted to play some board game or other. But I enjoyed the games much more whenever Fraser joined us. While Harriet pondered over every move he'd roll his heart-melting eyes at me and I'd burst out laughing: sometimes we were seized by uncontrollable fits of laughter. Harriet would frown at us distractedly but if she seemed upset Fraser immediately apologised. This used to amaze me. I had never wished for a sibling before I saw Fraser and Harriet together. He was utterly unlike any other child I knew - there was such gentleness in how he spoke, moved, ate – in everything he did.

Fraser loved all my stories, especially the ones about my French great-grandparents: a clown and a trapeze artist in a circus that was touring Ireland, they fell in love with Ballyboreen and quit the circus to become farm workers. Obviously, I never told him any of my mother's brutal stories.

From St Catherine's, Harriet went on to do medicine at Oxford and I started English Lit at Glasgow Uni, and loved everything about being a student. But my mother raged whenever I come home late: 'What hour of the night do you call this? I could be dead with the loneliness here on my own but you couldn't care less! I've worked my fingers to the bone to rear you and this is the thanks I get..."

In the middle of my second year, during yet another tirade about my selfishness and airs and graces since I'd become a 'Stuuuudent' I went to my bedroom, packed a rucksack and left.

Two friends who shared a flat in the west end let me kip on their sofa. I quit uni and got a job in a pub called The Right Note. At first I tried phoning home every night although the nearest working phone box was a mile away and there was always a queue, which meant a long wait, frequently in foul weather. But every time my mother heard me say, 'Hello?' she hung up.

Every Friday a soul band called Red Satin played in The Right Note. 'That trumpeter can't keep his eyes off you,' another barmaid started telling me, and I always told her she was imagining it – blokes who fancied me were never blessed with physique or looks.

But then one night, after Red Satin finished their set, the trumpeter came over to me and asked: 'Don't I recognise you from somewhere?' The limpest chat-up line ever but it didn't occur to me to answer sarcastically. Instead I shook my head.

What's your name?'

'Mary Tumulty.' I hated saying my name, so many people laughed at it.

'Mary Tumulty?' He didn't laugh. 'I don't know what it is, but there's something really familiar about you.'

'You see me here every Friday.'

'No, the very first night I saw you here, I was sure I recognised you from somewhere. Can I see you home?'

I nodded in surprise.

All the way home, he asked me about places I frequented. Gleeful that someone as gorgeous and talented as Colly was showing such interest in me, I wished my friends' flat was twenty miles away and we could keep on walking through the night, but we reached it all too soon. I longed to invite him in for coffee but didn't dare pushing my welcome in the flat. To my huge delight he asked: 'Can I walk you home again next week?'

He started walking me home every Friday. They can't all have been brilliantly moonlit nights but whenever I recall those walks I'm instantly transported back to the thrill of Colly tall and sheltering beside me, his beautiful profile, amazing hair, trumpet case strapped to his back, and his low voice tingling my skin as he talked about musicians I'd never heard of. Maybe my memories aren't reliable but they're crystal clear and those walks home with Colly were the most romantic nights of my life. Every time he said: 'Why do you seem so familiar to me?' I laughed with pure happiness.

One night Colly told me: 'My Mum's from Brazil, Fortaleza? She used to be a model but last year she moved back home to look after my grandmother. I'm hoping to visit her next year. I've never met my father. He was a fashion photographer. Mum only found out he was married when she told him she was pregnant.' He stated all this flatly as if giving his address. 'Then Mum met my step-dad when I was six. He was really into fishing and often took me with him.' Suddenly his voice was warm again: 'He was really into music too but couldn't play anything so he did all he could to encourage me.' Colly paused. 'He died three years ago. Heart attack -,'

'Oh Colly - ' but I couldn't think what to say. It always flummoxed me when people talked about fathers, as if they were recalling a holiday in a country too exotic for me to imagine.

One weekend Colly's flat-mate was away so he invited me to the flat 'for lunch and dot dot dot.' That's actually what he said. I was the most excited I've ever been that Saturday afternoon as I walked to his flat. On opening the door he pulled me inside and kissed me hotly. When I drew back from him, dizzy with happiness, I saw a much nicer living room than I'd expected. A huge bookcase had two shelves filled with LP's, the rest with books. Another wall was covered with black-and-white photos of mostly black men. 'Who are they?' I wondered.

'Seriously? You really want to know?'

'Definitely!'

'OK. That's Buddy Bolden from New Orleans. The first truly great jazz trumpeter. That's King Oliver – he was a huge fan of Buddy Bolden and helped spread jazz from New Orleans to Chicago. This of course is the best trumpeter ever, ever, ever, Satchmo himself,' Colly paused, 'How long have you got?'

'Forever!'

He laughed, shaking his head. 'It's so weird. It's like I've always known you –'

I had to look away, the tenderness in his voice was too much. That's when I saw the photograph of a red-haired man on the window sill. 'Who's he?'

'That's my step-dad.' Colly brought the photo over to me. I took it from him and stared at someone I'd never known yet recognised instinctively. He had my dimples. Goose-bumps rose on my arms.

'What's wrong, Mary?'

I couldn't speak.

'You recognise Al?'

Fraser was ten the first time he said to me: 'I'm marrying you when I grow up, Mary.'

'Do your parents know this?' I couldn't help laughing.

We were playing Monopoly and Harriet had gone to the kitchen for a glass of water.

'I don't need to tell anyone but you. I'm serious, Mary, I'm going to marry you,' he was watching me so gravely my laughter faded.

'No, Fraser. When you grow up you'll meet someone your own age and fall head over heels in love. I'm far too old for you.'

'No you're not.'

Harriet reappeared just then, and Fraser stared at the board with fierce concentration. My face burned as if I was guilty of something even though I knew I'd done nothing wrong. We continued the game and I kept losing while Harriet bought up half the board and won, as always.

Over the following years Fraser told me many times that he'd marry me when he grew up. I laughed every time and told him he'd meet someone else, someone totally stunning and gifted, and he always shook his head: 'No, Mary, I'll never love anyone more than I love you.'

I never told anyone of these 'proposals' (even calling them that seemed ridiculous). I presumed neither Harriet nor her parents were aware of Fraser's declarations and sometimes longed to tell her, but I'd have been mortified if she wanted evidence I wasn't making it up.

I didn't meet Harriet for some years after I left home but we continued corresponding regularly. Occasionally she mentioned

Fraser: he got a camera for his sixteenth birthday, became hooked on photography, went on to win some awards. Reading his name, I always felt a smile on my face as I imagined teasing him one day about how he used to propose to me.

The first I knew of Harriet's wedding was when the invitation arrived in the post with the PS 'Will you be my bridesmaid?'

I immediately phoned her to congratulate her and after dogged questioning found out that Raymond had recently joined her parents' dental surgery as a junior partner, and her parents happened to be on holiday when Harriet broke her two front teeth in a fall from her bike. So Raymond treated her and they found romance in the fitting of two crowns. 'I knew I wanted to marry him after an hour but waited a week to propose.'

My biggest shock at the wedding was seeing Fraser. The boy I'd expected was gone entirely, and I couldn't stop crying: 'I can't believe it's you!' But every time I wanted to tease him my throat dried up: he was too tall, too handsome. My voice squeaked when I tried: 'So where's your girlfriend today?'

'We broke up.' He smiled at me like we were sharing a secret. I blushed.

'Harriet told me you have a boyfriend?'

'Yes, but his band is touring Germany just now so he couldn't make it,' I sighed with more ruefulness than I felt.

'Are you very much in lo-

At that moment we were interrupted: Fraser was needed for a family photo. Otherwise I'd have assured him I was madly in love.

After the meal ended Fraser came and sat next to me, and asked: 'Any stories, Mary?'

By then I was a court reporter, and started telling him about the oddballs in a case I was covering. Fraser's laugh was deeper, but every bit as flattering as I remembered and I felt inordinately happy and comforted by being with someone who'd known me from childhood, and enjoyed hearing stories as much as I enjoyed telling them.

At the end of the evening Fraser stood with me on the hotel steps as I waited for my taxi and all the while we continued chatting like great old pals. When my taxi arrived he caught my elbow: 'Remember, Mary, we're getting married one day.'

'Oh Fraser!' I laughed, but my heart started pounding. I told myself I'd had too much wine.

I slid onto Colly's sofa and he sat next to me. 'That's who you remind me of! My step-dad! Your smile. Your laugh. Your dimples! You're his double. Jesus. This is too weird.'

'You're four years older than me. I was two when you were six,' I was frantically recalling what my mother had told me. As I'd got older I'd realised so many of her stories couldn't possibly be true but stupidly, stupidly, stupidly, I had never before doubted her account of my father's death. In a flash - not the lightening of a Damascene moment but a pitching into a blackout - I knew she'd made it up. 'Was he an alcoholic?' my voice shook.

'Al? No! He liked few pints every now and then, that's all. Why do you ask?'

'I need to talk to my mother. Sorry, Colly. I have to go. Now.' I stood up on rubbery legs.

He stood up and caught me, and I leaned into him gratefully and didn't argue when he said: 'I'm coming with you.'

After I pressed her door bell I gripped Colly's hand so hard it was bruised the next day. When my mother opened the door I saw her stiffen. 'What?' she glared at me.

'Can we come in?'

I thought she was going to shut the door on us but after a horrible pause she turned round and headed for the kitchen. I followed, leading Colly into what had once seemed the finest place in the world to me. My mother sat in her chair at the far side of the table and stared out the window. My chair, at the other side of the table, was gone. There was nowhere else to sit. Above the table was a rectangle of brighter wallpaper where the photograph of me on my first Communion used to hang.

I hadn't imagined a welcome but it felt like the air from her force-field was pounding me as I asked: 'What really happened to my father?'

'What good will knowing that do you?'

I knew how good she was at making arguments when she didn't want to answer something and said nothing.

'The bastard up and left me.

For a black whore.

When you were a baby.

Satisfied?'

When I recovered my voice I asked: 'So he never fell and banged his head and died?'

'More's the pity!'

'Have you any photos of him?'

'You're joking.'

'Is this him?' I took the photograph of Colly's step-father from my bag and walked over to her. She kept looking out the window so I pushed the photo right up in front of her face. 'Is that my father?'

'Where did you get that?'

'Is it him?'

Her lips clenched.

'Is it him, Ma? Please, Ma. Just answer that and I won't ask you another single question. I swear I won't.'

She shut her eyes, and then she nodded. 'Now go. Leave me alone.'

'My mother isn't black and she isn't a whore.' Colly said when we were back on the street. I knew I'd start crying if I tried to apologise. There was a whine in my head I couldn't stop: He chose you over me. He chose you over me. He chose you over me.

Colly took my hand and we started down the street. 'Back to my place?'

I nodded but I didn't want to go back to his place. As we walked hand in hand I kept veering between a longing to batter him until he collapsed, and a longing to be enfolded in his arms, sobbing my heart out. I couldn't speak, and we waited for the bus, then sat on it for forty minutes, in unbroken silence. Soon as we stepped off I started hurrying up the street.

'Mary! Wait!' he called after me.

'I'll see you later!' I shouted back.

I walked streets blindly. I knew my anger with Colly was irrational and worried that I was turning against him as unreasonably as my mother turned against people. So when Red Silk arrived that evening I gave Colly a big smile. For the first time he came over to me before they started playing: 'Wait til you hear tonight's set, Mary, six songs with totally new arrangements! You'll love it.'

'I can't wait,' I smiled at him stupidly, thinking: Aren't you going to ask me how I am?

He never asked me that. So I told myself he understood how devastated I was without asking, and wanted only to cheer me up.

No actual conversation I've ever had with Colly has been remotely as consoling as any of the millions I've imagined. That night the drummer from Red Satin gave us a lift back to Colly's flat and all the way there, the two of them raved about how well their new set had gone down. If only we were alone, I kept thinking, I could ask him all about my father.

Soon as we were inside his flat Colly started kissing and caressing and undressing me with all the passion I'd been fantasising about twelve hours earlier. After a while I gave up wishing he'd notice I wasn't responding and that I was trying to

170

edge away from him. So I lost my virginity. Afterwards, as we curled together in his single bed he started talking about the new songs all over again, repeating everything he'd already said in the van on the way home. Bad luck, I told myself, that he's so high about the set tonight. Any other time he'd surely notice how upset I am.

Stupidly, I expected Colly to understand how devastating it was for me he'd had my father all the years I thought him dead. Colly has never shown any awareness of that, and I've always failed to tell him. But for years I used to plead: 'Tell me something about my father.'

'What do you want to know?'

'Whatever comes into your head.'

'I've already told you: he was very patient and kind, very good to me and my mother. We were devastated when he died.'

'I know you've told me that Colly – but what was he really like?'

'Exactly like you.'

No matter how many times I asked what my father was like, 'Exactly like you,' was Colly's reply.

'How? In what way?' I'd persist desperately.

'Can't explain,' he'd yawn or sigh and drum his fingers, always a sign that he was bored.

The question that simmered eternally inside me but I never asked: 'Did he ever talk about me?'

Sometimes Colly mentioned my father when recalling gigs they'd gone to. His memory of gigs is phenomenal: perfect recall of every lyric, arrangement and key. 'Did my Dad enjoy it as much as you?' I'd interrupt, stressing 'my' – Colly always forgot Al was my father too.

'Of course.' Without missing a beat he'd continue reliving the gig, and I'd silently curse him.

Yet Colly has always been kind and generous to me. After Red Satin's first sell-out tour of Japan he figured he'd never lack money again and urged me to go back to university. Thanks to him I got my degree.

It has always amazed me how easily Colly says: 'I love you.' I'm far talkative than him but have never uttered those words. That's not all I've failed to utter in our thirty year marriage. Every time he listed all the arguments against having babies I failed to tell him how much I wanted one.

Once, as he was recalling yet another gig, I suddenly said: 'You don't actually love me at all.'

'Don't be so stupid, Mary. Of course I love you.'

'You might think so, Colly, but fundamentally you've no interest in me.'

'What the hell are you on about?' He leapt up from his chair. 'Chrissake! Why are you being horrible? That's a rotten thing to say!' He stormed from the room, slamming the door behind him.

Damn, I thought. Why did I say that? But I wasn't trying to be horrible. Follow him. Apologise, I urged myself. But I couldn't move. Half an hour later Colly came back and blithely asked me: 'Seen my watch anywhere?'

I helped him search for it as if I too had totally forgotten our spat.

When Red Satin did their first European tour I missed Colly so much I couldn't sleep. But during their next tour I felt a light-heartedness I'd forgotten was possible. The more Red Satin toured, the more the dread I used to feel at Colly's leaving and gladness at his return reversed.

It took me years to notice that whenever I talked to Colly for longer than a minute, he'd start yawning or sighing or drumming his fingers. One evening after I'd just listened to him rubbishing some band for an hour, this irked me even more than usual. 'You know what, Colly? Saying 'I love you,' means nothing if you get so bored every time I try telling you a story.'

'What?'

'Admit it: I bore you.'

'What the hell are you saying?'

I took a deep breath: 'We should separate.'

'No!' Tears filled his eyes. 'If you ever leave me I'll kill myself.'

Pain shot through me, searing, burning, stabbing pain. 'That's unforgivable, Colly,' I whispered.

'Don't push me then. Because I swear I mean it. I mean it, Mary. I couldn't live without you.'

Ever since, all my battles with him have been in my head. I often hate Colly, but then I hate myself for hating him. He's loyal and generous and easy going and occasionally loving, as long as I make no demands on his attention.

Harriet and Raymond live near Inverness now and I visit them every September. Colly never comes: he calls Harriet 'Miss Boring' even though they only met once, at my mother's funeral, (and apart from myself, Harriet and Colly, the only other mourners were two neighbours - not a soul from Ballyboreen). Harriet and I always go for long walks and her passion for flora and fauna is more enjoyable than card or board games. It's weird how our friendship has endured even though I've always thought myself closer to some other friends. But Harriet knows stuff about me that nobody else knows and I don't mind anymore that she's so reticent. Occasionally she mentioned Fraser, working in London ever since he qualified. Once I asked her: 'Is he seeing anyone?'

'He never tells me anything like that.' If she noticed my sudden blushing she made no comment.

I visited Harriet last weekend. When I got off the train in Inverness I heard 'Mary!' and was almost lifted from the ground in a hug.

'Fraser?' I drew back to look up at his face. All his curls were gone - he has a silver buzz-cut but his eyes are as beautiful as ever. 'What are you doing here? Harriet never said! When did you - I haven't seen you for - what? Thirty two years? You look so – I mean you - When did you – oh my God – I can't - ' Telling myself I was far too old for him wasn't working anymore. As I gabbled incoherently he put his hands on my shoulders, saying: 'Let me look at you,' and his eyes searched my face, making me feel like a rare diamond in the hands of a master jeweller. 'Mary,' he breathed, 'it's so good to see you.'

'Where's Harriet?' I asked in an effort to focus on someone else.

'At home. I insisted on meeting you, Mary.'

'Oh Fraser. I'm thrilled,' I laughed, desperately wanting to sound jokey. 'But come on, we can't stand here all day.' I needed to move before I was completely undone, and hurried for the exit. 'You're right, Mary,' he laughed, hurrying after me.

'There's my car,' he pointed to a silver car when we got outside.

I continued hurrying towards it, telling myself: get a grip, get a grip, get a grip.

As we got into the car I wondered what to ask first: was he married? With someone? Had he children? How long was he back for?

'Mary. I know I've no right – I know you're married and - '

Fastening my seatbelt, I said nothing.

'You always told me I'd fall in love with someone else.' I could feel him looking at me. 'I haven't. I've finally come to ask - if you say no, that's fine Mary. Obviously, if you're happy – I swear I won't say another word. But - Mary – if you're not happy? If – '

A year after I left home, I was working one night when two police women entered and one asked the barman near me: 'Is there a Mary Tumulty here?'

He pointed to me.

Approaching me, she asked softly. 'Could we have a word with you, hen?'

A neighbour became concerned after she hadn't seen my mother for a week. The police broke in and found her - she'd broken the glass pane above the bathroom door frame and looped the rope through it. 'Betrayed by one and all' was carved into the kitchen table - no other note was found.

Guilt has throbbed through me ever since. Sometimes now I can go almost a day without thinking about her but the ache is no less when I do.

'Oh God, Mary. Don't cry. Please, please, Mary. I'm sorry. I shouldn't have-'

'No, Fraser, no – it's not that – it's - ' but I couldn't explain anything to him – I was too happy and too distraught. I whispered: 'I love you,' and flinched. That wasn't what I meant to say. But I didn't know what I meant to say.

He cupped my chin and then we were clutching one another like we'd never, ever let go.

But it's no use. It's no use that as Fraser and I walked twenty miles together last weekend I felt more comforted than I've ever felt in my life. It's no use that he listened so attentively to me. It's no use that he let me talk and talk and talk like my mother. Nobody else has ever done that. It's no use that he offered to move anywhere, to live with me anywhere I want to live.

Last night I was at a gig with Colly. The singer introduced her last song with the story that inspired it: on her death bed, her 87 year-old great-aunt had beckoned to her husband of 69 years to come closer, then whispered to him with her last, dying breath: 'I should never have married you.'

The whole audience broke into laughter.

I laughed, too.

I laughed the loudest of all.

***

The Mart
Lela Tredwell

Lela Tredwell is a writer of fiction and non-fiction, a spirited creator and a Lecturer in English and History. A winner of the Fables for a Modern World Short Story Competition, she has also been shortlisted for The Bridport Prize 2013, commended in The Orwell Society's Dystopian Short Story Competition 2014 and longlisted in The Fish Publishing Short Story Prize 2015. Her essays of recommendation have been published by Thresholds Home of the International Short Story Forum. She enjoys writing a range of different forms of fiction: short stories, novels, flash fiction, poetry and writing for stage. She was recently awarded a Masters Degree in Creative Writing.

The Mart, Lela's entry to Aestas 2015, is a difficult yet compelling read. As Judge Clare Wallace puts it, "reading this story felt close, and uncomfortable, and as a reader, I was a fearful bystander, rubbernecking at something I wanted to turn away from but couldn't. It's unflinching, unenjoyable, and brilliantly accomplished."

After the quake felled the Supermart, Danny, Tag and Simon used to play in the abandoned car park around the mangled mass of concrete and steel. It had all been fenced off after the fall but nobody bothered to organise a clear up so the boys would climb over the chain link, landing like mongrel cats on the other side.

While they were still young enough they'd pretend they were cow boys, sheriffs in some desolate frontier of the Wild West. They never wore hats or anything; they weren't gay. But they held up their hands like guns and played out last stands, like they were Billy the fucking Kid, Sundance, Wyatt Earp.

Apparently Grace always wanted to be Annie Oakley but she was never allowed to play. Even when she proved she could scale the eight foot fence around the parking lot, Danny still told her to fuck off out.

"This." Danny growled, pointing decisively at the concrete lot. "Man territory. No women allowed."

So Grace took to standing on the outside of the fence and peering in through the gaps, like some strung up life-sized rag doll.

"Your sister creeps me out, mate, why doesn't she go home?" Tag tried saying to Danny one day, but Danny shrugged. Then out of nowhere he turned and shoved Tag so hard he tripped over his own feet and landed hard on his back bone.

"What the fuck, man?"

"Don't you fucking look at her, you hear? Don't you so much as look at her."

"Alright, man. I'm not looking. Jesus. You maniac."

Still she really used to give Tag the creeps. Just watching, staring in from the side lines, a player on the bench, waiting for a chance to get in the game. The audience put him off his stride and during the wide games he took to hiding behind broken bits of the store.

"Get out here, Sundance." Danny would say, "Why you hiding like a pouf?"

Then Shred joined them, and How, and Fetch, and the Wild West games started to feel silly. So they took to kicking things around the lot, running up and down like they were a relay team. Or else they'd just hang out on the steps of the crumpled building, where older still, they smoked weed. They took then to seeking out shards of glass from the Supermart windows, some still in place sticking up like confused icicles, and smashing them with stones or lengths of wood, the building's broken bones. The sound went bouncing off the rubble and around the lot.

Word spread. Soon there was a big bunch of the neighbourhood hanging out there. They called themselves 'The Beast Boys' for a while; then later on, when it was judged to be a bit lame they just said 'those that go down The Mart'.

Through it all, Grace remained on the outside. Outside of the fence staring in with a forlorn rag doll look on her face. As they got older some of the boys would go over and try to talk to her, maybe jeer at her through the metal. If Danny was out of ear shot they'd suggest sexual things they'd want to do to her, but never if Danny was nearby. He was too unpredictable. A lot of the kids were scared of him. He seemed capable of anything. At school he roamed the corridors crashing into anyone he didn't like the look of. Rarely any of the Mart crew. But no one knew when that might change.

One Thursday after school Grace came down the ruin but there was no sign of Danny. Grace didn't seem to know where he was. Or if she did, she wasn't telling. Some of the pack took this as a chance to up their sexual suggestions to more graphic and violent slurs. But still Grace stood on the outside of the fence, gawking in.

Danny wasn't there on the Friday either.

While the others were occupied with chasing a seagull who'd grabbed at some kid's bacci, Tag went over and tried reasoning with Rag Dolly Gracie.

"You don't have to come here when Danny's not around."

Grace didn't say anything.

"I mean, you can stay at home."

He wondered then if Grace was deaf and none of them had ever noticed. Perhaps she read lips and he hadn't enunciated well enough. He tried again, slower this time. He tried hard to move his lips.

"You can go home, Grace."

She just stared at him like he was an anomaly, a blot on the landscape.

Danny wasn't there Monday either. In fact he didn't show up at The Mart all week. On Thursday Guffer took out his cock and waved it at Grace. Then, when she didn't react, he started pissing through the links of the chain, the arch of hot urine splashing Grace's jelly shoes. She jumped back just far enough not to get pissed on any further. A couple of other guys joined Guffer, laughing, shaking the drops of pee out of themselves over the concrete. Some of the spray caught in the chain link and hung off the metal in little beads of acid rain.

Tag scanned her face wanting to see some sign of emotion. He realised he had a dark deep longing to see her cry. More than that. It was hard to admit to himself, but he wanted to be the one to make Rag Dolly Gracie sob.

Danny came back to The Mart the next week. He said he'd got some virus from his Uncle Fuckface who worked in a pharmacy. He said it was probably some kind of Planet of the Apes shit he'd managed to fight off. Lucky for all of them.

Danny didn't say anything about the pissing. He probably didn't know about it. Tag couldn't imagine he'd have stayed quiet if he did. Unless he was plotting some kind of secret revenge on Guffer, but that wasn't really Danny's style. Danny was more the sudden screaming rage kind of guy. If he had a problem with you, you knew about it right away.

To his horror, in bed at night, Tag started to plan ways he might get Grace to cry. He plotted out things he might say to goad her, then ways he might physically push at her, shove her down, bite, scratch, shake, smack her across parts of her skin, her soft flesh beneath. Sometimes in these scenarios she'd fight back, like a phoenix, overpowering him and laying into him, in the way he'd imagine Danny might, if he ever found out Tag was thinking about his sister this way. At other times she'd be docile, like a doll, limply let him do whatever he wanted. Either way he'd usually end these fantasies by fucking her. Sometimes she'd like it. Mostly, she wouldn't.

Danny got moved into Tag's Religious Studies class at school. Rumour had it he'd been hiding a substitute teacher's lunch above the ceiling tiles and given her a nervous breakdown. The story seemed to fit; Tag's teacher spoke to Danny in a kind of threatening way that suggested he was watching him pretty closely. Mr Strokes was six foot four and built like an industrial chimney. It seemed to do the trick.

They sat next to each other and Tag watched Danny draw penises on the dioramas of religious buildings, but only in places they'd be unlikely to be found: inside a crypt, at the top of an archway, behind a pillar. It suggested that Danny had a subtlety Tag hadn't before credited to him.

Danny generally flew under the radar in RS and Tag thought this was even more evidence of the lunch prank. He could have just asked Danny if he'd done it, but somehow he never found the right words. Besides, Tag reckoned it was taking all Danny's energies to determine where to hide his next drawing of an erect dick.

When they moved on to looking at Catholicism, Mr Strokes explained how Hell worked, what you had to do to go there, what got poked where by the devil when he got his hands on a sinner.

"Is it a sin to fuck your family, sir?" Danny asked, and the rest of the class laughed. Tag joined them.

"Do you mean to behave disrespectfully to your family, Danny?" Mr Strokes said as the giggles subsided.

"No, like fuck them, fuck them."

The class exploded with a roar. This time Tag held back. He could see Danny wasn't laughing.

"Incest?" said Mr Strokes.

When Danny didn't answer, he added, "Yes, that's a sin."

Tag noticed Danny didn't draw a lot of penises after that, erect, dripping or otherwise. Perhaps it had just been a phase. Tag tried drawing a tiny one inside the back cover of his RS book and showed it to Danny, but Danny just shrugged and said, "Gay."

Before the term ended for summer a community group got their claws into The Mart. They boarded up the worst of the ruin and got some school kids to paint murals on the wooden wall. A rainforest with various oddly shaped half hidden animals went up. Guffer pissed on a baboon, its head like a coconut peering out from behind tall grass.

When the crew tried ripping the wood down, the council put up CCTV cameras and had alarms installed. The posters said it was for the safety of children, that a clear up was underway. The headmaster at Tag's school announced in assembly how responsible the community group was; it was a wonder that the council had allowed the ruin to remain for so long. He said that now it was going to be safe to walk around at night and wasn't that a relief. He named a couple of kids in year nine who were involved with the group clearing up The Mart. Before the end of morning break they were paste. One had to go home because his nose wouldn't stop bleeding and the other went to A&E with suspected concussion.

With The Mart gone the crowd of regulars thinned out.

There were some feeble efforts to hang outside MacDonald's but the staff in their dorky caps chased them off with mangy mayonnaise. The problem with the park was that it was frequented by dog walkers; for exposure this was as bad as the CCTV. Tag realised his town didn't have enough suitably wide pavements to hang out on the street and no parent would tolerate such a crowd. Tag's mother had her nail painting business at home so there was no hope there, even if he'd wanted to invite the crew into his house, which he realised he didn't. It was altogether too embarrassing to show anyone else how you lived. You never knew what ammunition they might find among your things.

Once summer really got going, it turned out to be a searing one – sticky and close. Tag took to wandering the streets in the hope he might bump into someone worth talking to. Once he found Danny kicking over a rubbish bin. The pair went and sat on the steps of the Assembly Hall and threw bits of someone's discarded kebab at pigeons. They didn't say much. Tag liked to think they didn't have much left to share after all the Religious Studies lessons together, where they were coerced by Mr Stokes to talk about their beliefs on commandments, ethics and afterlives.

Danny grunted as he threw the food and that was enough communication for Tag. He realised then that he quite liked Danny. It seemed a strange thing to admit to himself after so many years down The Mart. He thought that given they'd started the place, there might just be an indissoluble bond between them. Simon had been there at the beginning too, of course. Someone said he'd gone gay - though Tag didn't believe it. There'd been a series of poundings from Guffer though, so Simon's Gran had moved the family away.

Danny and Tag, though, they were the core, really. And Gracie. Tag still thought about her, but his fantasies were different now he didn't see her every day. He almost asked Danny how she was now, but then an obese balding security guard shouted at them to fuck off and hobbled after them holding a stick. Tag didn't think the guy'd use it but they ran all the same.

"Bald, bastard!" said Tag as they caught their breath down the alleyway behind Blockbusters. Suddenly Danny punched the brick wall behind them. His fist crumpled up and he wrung it out in the air. Tag waited for an explanation.

"That was my Uncle Fuckface," he said still wincing slightly.

"I thought he was in a pharmacy," said Tag.

"He lost that job. They said he tried to take a lost girl home with him."

"Dick," said Tag. It seemed like the only response.

"Yeah. You remember Hell?" asked Danny.

It seemed a genuine question, so Tag said, "Yeah, I remember."

"He's getting the pitchfork fuck alright."

Danny laughed with a snort, rather aggressively. Tag laughed too. And soon they both were trying to hold back hysterics. Though, Tag suspected, neither of them knew quite what was so funny.

Walking through his estate one afternoon, Tag was fantasizing about bumping into Danny again, though he wasn't proud to realise it.

"Oi, Chase, get the fuck up here!"

Only Guffer called Tag, Chase. He seemed to think he was being clever, or funny perhaps, or just wanting things his way, with the suggestion that Tag wasn't entitled to his own name. He looked around to see a head disappearing through an upstairs window. A hand waved out beckoning.

Tag stopped walking but didn't make a move to the house. In time Guffer's face appeared. He looked flushed.

"I ain't gonna ask you twice, Chase!"

Tag had never liked Guffer but he knew that he wasn't a guy you wanted to keep waiting. He was a big build – the kind you weren't sure whether it was muscle or fat – and he liked to exercise his fists and piss on little girls.

The front door to Guffer's place wasn't locked so Tag went in unaided. He hadn't been inside the house before but the stairs were in the hallway, as they were with all the houses on the estate. The smell of deep fat frying and coffee and cat food was particular to Guffer's. The carpet on the stairs was worn out in places and for reasons he couldn't explain Tag tried to avoid those spots.

Guffer was standing at the top on the landing, looking triumphant. He didn't seem to be able to keep still.

"Come on, bitch, hurry up, though it ain't going nowhere."

"What?" said Tag. He wanted to add, I ain't your bitch, but knew it would be a basic mistake. He didn't have an easy escape route.

Tag followed Guffer as he strutted into a bedroom painted entirely black, even the radiator. The heavy curtains were pulled most way across the window now so the lighting was limited. Still Tag was distracted by the thick smell that mixed with the stench of Guffer's house. Guffer had shut the window to a crack so no oxygen was rushing in. On the near wall Tag could just about make out a graphic Limp Bizkit poster with a blonde woman touching herself while riding a serpent. The floor was littered with dirty laundry and soiled food receptacles.

"You're it, Chase," Guffer laughed and he left the room slamming the door behind him. Later Tag would reflect on how long Guffer must have been storing that line, stalling for what he felt was the perfect moment.

A scratching from a shelf on the wall turned out to be a rat partially buried in sawdust at the bottom of its cage. It seemed likely the thing was gnawing on sunflower seeds as a large jar of them stood next to it, on the other side of the bars.

In the far corner of the room was Guffer's bed. Black sheets, of course. That's how Tag first made out the whiteness of her feet, shining stars in each bottom corner of the mattress. The mangled duvet had fallen on the floor. He tried moving in, only for his foot to come into contact with a crumbed plate that clattered against a knife.

She was naked from the waist down.

He remembered driving with his mother to the coast when there'd been a road accident up ahead. As they got nearer to the flicking neon blue that distorted the bank, the rest of the road and the sky, his mother had told him not to look. Only he hadn't been able to help himself and had seen the man lying in the road, the ambulance men working him over, getting ready to cover him up.

Guffer was thundering down the stairs, he heard him. Had he been listening outside the door? It seemed most likely. But time too was skewed.

Through the window now he heard Guffer's voice shouting down the neighbourhood, calling in estate boys, some of them from the Mart crew probably, some of them older still. Tag knew the kind of people Guffer associated with. Simon hadn't had a chance.

Pounding started on the stairs. Ascending footsteps.

Tag moved further towards the bed even though an instinct told him not to. He could see Grace's eyes were shut tight and she was pushing her fingernails from her left hand into the flesh on her thumb. It was like an open fist. He wanted to haul up the duvet and wrap Grace in it but he also didn't want to reach over her. The risk he would run of touching her skin was too great.

This wasn't how it was supposed to go. Or maybe it had been once, but now he was staring at the scene for real, he wanted to puke.

How long was it supposed to take?

He waited.

Standing there, her made an attempt to scan Guffer's room for something that might enable him to be chivalrous, rescue Grace from Guffer's foul stinking pit, take her where the others wouldn't be able to spew their hot spunk over her, take her back to being Rag Dolly Gracie, or back further still to Annie Oakley. To a time long before they all started on her, when they could still have let her join in the games.

A sweet tin in the shape of a robot

A bent plastic sword

A board game of Kurplunk

It was a futile search. Beating his way out of here with Gracie wasn't an option. Even if Danny had been here they wouldn't have reached as far as the top of the stairs before they were paste. And the gang outside would do whatever they planned to do to Gracie anyway. He knew that.

Guffer's broad checked shirt was decorating the head of the bed.

Would he know that Tag hadn't done it? Tag was no great actor. Besides he didn't even know how he should look after such an act.

He unzipped his fly, fumbling with the button at the top.

"Gracie," he whispered at her. "Grace, are you alright?"

It was a stupid question and he wasn't surprised when Grace didn't reply. Why would she? Years later he would think she was probably already too far away to hear him calling to her.

"Grace, I'm not going to…"

He trailed off.

Someone banged on the door.

"Turn's over, Chase, bitch, get out!"

Tag grabbed the waist band of his jeans and shook them. He picked his way gingerly back to the door while the rat raced up the side of its cage, claws ringing out over the bars. The door yielded to his sweaty hand on the knob.

Outside, there was a line of older kids from the estate just as he had suspected. They leered at him. Tag zipped up his fly as one of them pushed past him into Guffer's room. The door shut with a thump and the assembled company cheered. As he walked towards the top of the stairs Guffer moved forward and held up a hand. The hanging high five initiated a wrenching inside. Choking back the bile that rose suddenly, Tag half raised his hand and curled his fingers into a fist. Giving a weak thumbs up, he trudged down the stairs, heart hammering against his rib cage.

There was nowhere else to go.

***

White Wings
Mark Patton

Mark Patton was born on the island of Jersey in 1965. He grew up there, studied Archaeology and Anthropology at Cambridge, and completed his PhD at University College London in 1990. He now lives in London, and is the author of three historical novels, all published by Crooked Cat Publications: Undreamed Shores (2012), An Accidental King (2013) and Omphalos (2014). He blogs regularly on aspects of history and historical fiction at http://mark-patton.blogspot.co.uk.

White Wings, Mark's entry to Aestas 2015 is a piece of historical fiction based on the Grosvenor, a merchant ship that sank off the coast of South Africa in 1782. Judge Wallace says "This story was inspired by real events, which are fascinating. I thought the quality of the writing and the plot were strong."

Let me tell you how it happened. It is a story now, but it was real at the time. The winds howled through the village all night, first in one direction, then in another. They lifted the thatch of the houses and threw the grain baskets and the milking buckets around in the air. It was almost daylight when the winds began to die down, and I was finally able to get some sleep.

The next thing I knew, my daughter, Damza, was shaking me. "*Yho*, Father, come quickly. There is something in the bay, like a house that floats, and there are men in the sea, coming on to the beach."

I threw a cloak around my shoulders, picked up my spear and shield and stepped out into the half-light.

Damza's half-sister, Mityi, waited outside. "We had gone down to the shore to gather mussels," she said, "and then we saw it, and we saw the men, and we were afraid, so we ran back here."

"You did right," I replied. "It is dangerous to show yourself to men you do not know. Let me lead the way, in case we meet them on the path."

We walked swiftly and, when we reached the waterfall, I saw it. A mass of wood rising and falling on the waves, swathes of white cloth falling around it into the sea, timber shattered on the rocks.

"Have you ever seen anything like it?" Mityi asked.

"I have seen such things on the horizon, those white cloths billowing out above it like pelican wings, but they have always been in the distance, like whales. I have never seen such a thing so close."

As the sun rose above the horizon, I saw that the thing was breaking up on the rocks. Two men were in the sea, moving through the water, the way hippos do. They had ropes, like cattle-tethers, that they were trying to bring ashore. Other people, women as well as men, separated from one another by the waves, called to each other in a strange tongue.

"*Tyhini*, Father, what are they?" asked Damza. "Perhaps they are evil spirits, like *Hlanganyana*, who eat human flesh."

"*Hlanganyana* exists only in stories. He is not real. These are people, but you should not get close. Come, let us go back to the village. We must tell our grandfathers of this, and hear what they have to say."

I'd seen the coast, as clear as anything, from the foretop of the *Grosvenor*. I'd shouted it out for all to hear. After I got down, I described the rocky shore to the officer of the watch, Mr Shaw. He thanked me, and called to his mate, Bill Habberley, to put the helm a-lee. But then the captain came on to the deck with another of the officers, Mr Beale, and asked what was going on.

"We are miles from any land," Beale scoffed. "Who said he'd seen land?"

I stepped forward to speak, but he waved me away. "The man's mad. Either that or he's had too much rum."

The captain spat on the deck. "Put the ship about again, Mr Beale."

Mr Shaw and his mate went down below, muttering to each other, and I quickly followed. Of all the officers, Mr Beale was never the one to spare the lash. I called to Mr Shaw, but he ignored me, hurrying back to his cabin. Damn them all if they wouldn't listen. It wasn't my ship, or my cargo, or my fancy passengers in the roundhouse with their airs and graces.

The cry for all hands went up in the middle of the night. Bill Habberley came below to tip us out of our hammocks.

"What's happening, Mr Habberley?" I asks.

"Why, we are on a lee-shore, you fool! The captain needs everyone on deck to haul the ship off the rocks."

"That'll be the shore I spotted and told them about," I said to the man next to me. "The one Mr Beale and the captain kept steering towards."

Passengers and crew crowded together on the deck. A man pointed along a moonbeam, which lit up the waves breaking at the foot of a cliff. Bill Habberley did his best to herd the passengers below, whilst Mr Shaw directed us to take up the ropes. The captain called for silence. He shouted orders to Mr Beale at the helm. "Keep her full again for stays … let go the anchor …put down the helm!"

The ship lurched suddenly. The yards swung around and canvas flapped in the air above us. I looked up, waiting for the wind to fill the sails once again. There was a crunch from below, and a violent shudder.

"We're aground," said Mr Shaw, turning to the captain. "What now."

The captain peered over the rail. "It's only a matter of time before she starts to break up." He looked up at the mainmast, sweat rolling from his face. "Take it down."

The bosun thrust an axe into my hand and, with half a dozen of my shipmates, we set to work. We laboured through the night, taking down the mainmast and the foremast, cutting up the spars and lashing the pieces together to make a raft.

The bosun and his mates lowered the raft into the foaming water, and threw ropes over the side of the ship for us to clamber down. There must have been a dozen of us on that raft, with only planks to use as paddles. We pushed away from the side of the ship and made for the coast. No sooner were we afloat than the timbers beneath us began to creak and groan. The raft was sinking beneath our weight, and the waves washed over us. Men cried out as they slipped into the sea, but there was nothing I could do to help. A sharp jolt flung me forward, toppling me into the water. I thought I was lost but, as I called out to God, my prayer was answered. My feet sank into soft sand, whilst my head was still above the water. I hauled myself out onto the beach.

-

"It has happened once before," said Sipho, my father's brother. "It is only a story now, because nobody alive is old enough to remember it."

He sat for a moment, deep in thought, running his fingers around the head of his walking stick. Then he looked up. "Which boy in the village shall we say is the fastest runner?"

"My brother's son, Baibile," I suggested.

"Then let him run to the village of my cousin, Maduba, and fetch his wife, Makori. She may be able to speak to these people, since her mother was one who came out of the sea. For the moment, we will slaughter a goat and take it to the sea-people, since they must be in need of food. We cannot feed many people for many days, so we must send them on their way, but we should not send them away hungry. If any are sick or injured, we will take care of them, as my uncle's people took care of Makori's mother."

I slaughtered a goat, gutted it and lashed its feet to a pole. I took one end of the pole, and my son, Mbulu, took the other, as we set off for the beach. My wives and daughters followed behind with a great many of the villagers, since everyone was now talking about the sea-people.

As we approached the bay, I saw that the people had come up from the beach onto the grass around the river-mouth. They had made a shelter from some of the wood and white cloth. Some men were sitting around a fire, whilst others slept on the ground. A man in blue clothes with golden buttons walked up and down, talking first with one person and then with another. I pointed him out to Mbulu.

"I think he must be their chief. We will give the goat to him."

I called to Geza, my right-hand wife, who carried my spear and shield. "Stay back here with the women and the small children. Take care of our weapons, for we do not want these people to feel afraid."

Those men who carried weapons handed them to their wives, who sat down on the grass with Geza, gathering the little ones around them.

As Mbulu and I walked towards the man in blue, all of the sea-people stopped talking, and stared at us. The man in blue reached to his belt and unsheathed a long metal knife, which he brandished towards us, its deadly blade glinting in the sunlight.

"Put the goat down," I whispered to Mbulu, "and step back."

We laid the goat on the ground, and I showed the palms of my hands to the man in blue, and then pointed to the goat. He returned his knife to its sheath, but then he went back to his conversation with his companions, ignoring both us and the goat. Mbulu's fist clenched in anger.

"Be calm," I whispered. "Do not provoke these men to come at us with their knives."

As we walked down to the beach, most of the sea-people ignored us, as their chief had done. There were a few women and children, but Mbulu counted sixty men. "A good reason why we must not fight with them," I insisted.

The beach was strewn with wood. One of the village boys picked up a piece, and ran up to me in great excitement. "Look," he said. "There is iron!"

The plank he was holding was studded with long iron pins.

"Can we gather it?" He asked.

None of the sea-people seemed to be taking any interest in it, so I nodded. "Take care, though," I warned, "since they have knives. If they challenge you, you must put it down."

The boys spent much of the day gathering the wood, and making a pile of it to burn, so that we would be left with only the iron, which the village smith could forge into knives, spear-points and ploughshares. None of the sea-people seemed to have any objection.

There was just one of these people who did not ignore us, a man of about thirty summers, with red, sun-burned skin, as they all had, and hair the colour of ripened millet. He approached us, his right hand outstretched. I extended my hand to him in a similar gesture, and greeted him. He said something to me that sounded like a greeting, although we could not understand each other's words. In his left hand, he held something like a calabash, but made of a brown material that reflected the sunlight. He drank from it, and handed it to me. I took a sip, and it tasted good, fruity, spicy, like nothing I had tasted before. I passed it to Mbulu, who also drank from it.

"Remember this man," I said to Mbulu. "We must find him again when Makori arrives."

–

Captain Coxon ignored the goat that had been laid at his feet by the men he and the other officers called "savages." It lay on the ground all day, attracting flies, until I fetched the ship's cook, Antonio, and together we plucked up the courage to approach Mr Habberley, to ask if we might take and cook it.

"If you wish to eat carrion," he sneered, "you are welcome to it."

"They don't seem like savages to me," I said to Antonio, as we carried it away. "Savages wouldn't bring us food. Surely we'd be their food."

He laughed. "Perhaps they are just fattening us up."

"I shared a bottle of port with a couple of them this morning, and they seemed friendly enough."

"Just keep that bottle hidden from the officers unless you want a flogging. The captain keeps the port for himself. If there's any left, I'll share it with you after sunset. A last taste of home!"

We shared the goat among the foremast-men, and it revived our spirits wonderfully. We'd all become fed up with salt pork during the voyage from Trincomalee, and the Malayan sailors won't touch the stuff. They'd been eating nothing but bread and lentils until this goat appeared. Even the steward, Henry Lilburne, smelt the roasting meat and asked if he could join us. He brought us two fine bottles of wine. His gossip about the goings on in the captain's tent gave us all much food for thought.

"The captain is practically at war with Mr Shaw and Mr Beale. He is determined that we should walk south. He thinks we can reach the Dutch colony at the Cape within a couple of weeks, but they can't agree on the route to take. I reckon most of the men would rather stick with Mr Shaw than with the captain."

"Mr Shaw is the better man on the sea," I says, "but here on land, he don't know his way any better than the rest of us."

Mr Lilburne shrugged. "We don't need to obey any of them anyhow. Our pay stopped when the ship was lost. It's every man for himself now we're ashore."

"What if we do reach the Dutch colony?" someone asked. "With England and Holland at war, surely we'd be clapped in irons?"

"For a few weeks, perhaps," says Lilburne, "but I reckon we'd be ransomed, and bound for London in no time."

A couple of the men started up a song – "In London town there lives a maid …"

I walked away. I felt the bile rising in my gullet. Since God had seen fit to free me from a gaol in London, as he had freed Saint Paul, I was not about to walk into another at the Cape. The memories of that night in Newgate came flooding back. The shouts and jeers of the crowd. The crackle and blood-red glow of the flames. The drunkards, with blue cockades in their hats, opening the door to my cell with the keys they had taken from the warder. My mad run through the streets as piles of furniture burned all around me, with only one thought, to reach the docks and enlist in the crew of a ship, any ship, even if it meant being pressed. The Navy, it was said, looked after its own. And now, in just a few weeks' time, a Dutchman, might take a fat bribe from the East India Company and put me on a ship for London. He'd think he was doing me a favour, when really he would be sending me off to Tyburn. I didn't sleep that night. I hadn't come this far to go back to London and swing.

In the morning I walked to the river to draw water. Looking up through the mist towards the waterfall, I saw a party of the natives coming towards me, dressed, as they had been before, in robes made from animal skins. As they drew closer, I recognised the man I had shared a drink with the previous day. He carried a shield and spear, but he did not threaten me with his weapon, as the captain had threatened him with his sword. Instead, he handed it to a woman beside him, and extended his hand to me as he had done before, although we still did not shake hands. He sat down on the riverbank, and gestured to me to sit beside him. An old woman came forward and joined us, whilst the other natives hung back. She was a little paler than the other natives, her hair greyer. Her chest was bare, and her breasts sagged. As she smiled at me, I saw that one of her front teeth was missing.

"Who are you?" she asks, in plain English! "Where do you come from?"

"My name is Joshua. I come from London. Where did you learn to speak English?"

She grinned. "London," she repeated, shaking her head. "Long, long ago, and far, far away, my mama ..." She paused, and pointed out to sea.

"Your mama came from London?"

She giggled like a little girl. "Perhaps."

"What did she tell you about the place she came from?"

"Long, long ago, and far, far away!"

The man said something to her in his own odd language, with a click after every word, and she replied, using many more words than she seemed to know in English. Then she turned to me again.

"There are men like you, from far away. Walk ten days ..." she pointed along the coast to the north. North. She was pointing north!

The man suddenly looked up, and jumped to his feet. The native men behind him lifted their spears, as if preparing for a fight.

I looked around and saw Mr Beale and his mate approaching us. Beale had his pistol drawn.

"Come away," he shouts. "The captain wishes to address the crew."

"Don't shoot them," I says. "The natives mean us no harm." But, when I looked around, I saw that they were already retreating up the hillside.

I followed Mr Beale to the tent that the officers had improvised from sailcloth and broken spars for the ladies to sleep in. The crates and barrels that had been saved from the wreck were stacked around the edges of the tent, and the passengers sat on them as the crewmen mustered before them. The captain strode out of the tent, and addressed us as like a candidate at the hustings. He announced his intention to lead us south, to the Cape. It would be a long and arduous journey through rough terrain, harassed by hostile savages, perhaps even preyed upon by cannibals, and certainly by wild beasts, but we were British, and known for our fortitude in the face of adversity so, with God's help, we would surely prevail. "God save the King!"

I'm sure he expected us to respond with a "huzzah!" but nobody did. As I glanced at the ladies sitting on the barrels in their fine, but now sodden, silk dresses, I saw their faces become more pallid with every word he spoke.

Mr Shaw stepped forward, and asked if any of us had anything we wished to say. The ship having been lost, we were all equals now, and the lowliest hand had his right to a say. There was silence. I stood up, and Mr Shaw gestured me to the front.

"I have spoken with the natives," I says, loud and clear so that everyone could hear. "One of them speaks some words of English. Her mother was from London. She says there is a settlement to the north, only ten days walk away ..."

"What nonsense is this?" asked Mr Habberley.

"The man is mad," said Mr Beale, addressing the captain. "I know him of old, a most surly and ignorant fellow. I found him sitting with the savages, and I heard their gabbling, amongst which I could discern not a word of English. If the savages pointed to the north, it is surely a trap to ensnare us. I say we go south with the captain."

At this, several people cheered, and I saw the smile spreading across the captain's red face. Someone threw a pebble, which hit me on the cheek. Some of the men started singing "Rule Britannia," and soon everyone had joined in. I had no chance of being heard above them, so I slipped away. I found the place in the wood where I had hidden the port bottle, and took a deep draught.

I stayed away from the rest of the crew and passengers, as they feasted on the remaining provisions, and prepared for their journey south.

As evening closed in, the natives passed by me, carrying the bounty they had gathered from the beach. The woman who had spoken to me in English wore a necklace that must have been washed ashore from the wreck. I smiled at her, then noticed the man who had introduced us, so to speak. I stood up, greeted him, and handed him the bottle. He took a drink, and passed it back to me. Leaving the crew and passengers of the *Grosvenor* behind, I followed the natives up the hill.

--

"Does he mean to come with us?" Mbulu whispered to me.

"It seems so," I replied. "He has a liver, to leave his companions and come away with people he does not know, whose language he cannot speak."

Geza made up a bed for him that night in one of the village store-huts. Makori and her husband shared their meal with him, but she could speak only a few words of his language, since her mother and aunt were so young when they came out of the sea all those years ago.

The following day, this man walked down with us to the beach, and we saw that most of his companions had left. We could tell from the tracks that they had gone south. We found just one man who had been left behind, because his leg was injured. Our red-faced friend tended his wound, and we helped him back to the village. Over the weeks, these men became like the gum and the bark. They could talk to one another in their own language, and we could listen, and try to learn from them, as they also learned our language. We called the first man Jikela, and the second Jongephi, since we could not pronounce their names in their own language.

We ate well that season, because Jikela and Jongephi came down to the beach with us every day, and helped us to find things, including great wooden boxes of meat which stayed fresh if you knew how to treat it, and lengths of fine, brightly coloured cloth, which our wives made into gowns. Jikela had a fine hand for wood-working. He found a box of tools on the beach, and used them to make wooden bowls and boxes, and yokes for the cattle. We had never had so much iron in the village.

Their companions did not fare so well. They split into different groups as they moved south. I do not know whether any survived but, each time we met relatives from the south, we heard of some who had starved, whose skeletons were found in the bush. There is not much to eat there if you have neither cattle nor crops, and cannot hunt, and have no knowledge of which plants are good to eat, and which ones are poisonous. My cousin now wears the blue coat that belonged to the chief of the sea-people. One of the starving men took refuge in his village. They gave him food, but he went into the cattle enclosure and took a shit on the grave of my cousin's father, so they drove him out, and no one knows what became of him.

Time passed, and both Jikela and Jongephi came to speak our language quite well. Jikela married Damza, and Jongephi married Mityi. Both girls became pregnant. One gave birth to a daughter, the other to a son.

"It will happen again, child of my brother," said Sipho. "It will be a story for our grandchildren to tell their grandchildren. Each year, we see more of their white pelican wings on the horizon. We were wise to take these men in, as Maduba's father took in Makori's mother and aunt when they came out of the sea as children. Some day, those people will come here, and we will be better prepared if our stories can be told in their tongue, as well as in our own."

***

Dragon Bird of Liaoning
Wilson F. Engel III

Dr. Wilson F. Engel, III, sometimes writing under the pseudonym E. W. Farnsworth, is widely published on line and in print. He is the author of seven books of poetry (four illustrated by artist Charlene S. Engel), two novels, a critical edition, numerous stories, a film script, a play, and over 250 literary essays, articles, notes and reviews. More information on his current and forthcoming works can be found at www.ewfarnsworth.com. Born in California, Dr. Engel now lives and writes in Arizona, USA. He is the Leverhulme Professor of Literature at the University of Edinburgh, Scotland, and is listed in The Directory of American Scholars.

Set in the Chinese province of Liaoning, the following story chronicles a paleontologist's search for a mythical bird. Judge Brett Alan Sanders feels "the mythology at the story's core is quite intriguing; and some of the descriptions, particularly of the Dragon Bird model and the live bird's flight, are very nice."

$\mathbf{D}$r. Phyllis Standish was a paleontologist on a mission. Her professional triumph was proving that living specimens of the coelacanth could still be found on earth after having been catalogued as extinct for 65 million years. In the Nineteen Seventies, a West Indian Ocean fisherman had boated this strange fish without releasing it, and the fish had subsequently made headlines. Then another living specimen was found and a third. The biological scholarly community was dumbfounded by these finds. Some might have wanted to bury the evidence quietly, but they had no way to suppress the truth once the living specimens had been verified and published in the popular media. Now Dr. Standish was conducting a similar investigation into a creature the Chinese paleontologists had named the dragon bird, whose fossilized remains were discovered in the Chinese province of Liaoning.

The dragon bird was a dinosaur with the features of an avian. Specifically, the many fossilized specimens clearly indicated that the dinosaur had feathers. Whether the dragon bird could fly was doubtful because of the enormous bulk of the body as compared with the small scale of the wings. What made Dr. Standish take notice was the linkage between the dragon bird fossils and the ancient Chinese myths about dragons, which were, like phoenixes, imperial emblems so faithfully rendered that they seemed to be alive. So instead of starting her work in the paleontologist heaven of Liaoning, Dr. Standish had decided to take a survey of the image and iconography of the dragon throughout Chinese history. She did this because her hypothesis was that the dragon bird was not extinct. Like the coelacanth, the dragon bird was, the paleontologist reasoned, still alive on earth but no evidence had been adduced to prove that fact, at least not yet.

Dr. Standish was on a quest to discover not yet another fossil of the dragon bird but a living specimen. Because all the pertinent fossil remains were unearthed in Liaoning did not necessarily mean that the feathered beasts were limited to that region exclusively. In fact dragon lore was a worldwide phenomenon in literary terms. She knew she might find her living specimen in nearly any habitat of the globe: on land, in caverns, in lakes or oceans, in the air or in some combination of those.

Her research assistant and graduate student Yangtze Su had long ago caught the infectious energy of the doctor's undertaking, and for the last three years she had scoured the oldest Chinese records for the evidence her major professor needed. From the records she made an enormous spreadsheet that allowed her to correlate the data about each reference to the imperial dragon and every representation of dragons from the earliest, crude forms to contemporary costumes used in street festivals throughout China on major holidays. She also traveled extensively to photograph images on former palace buildings and bronze public statuary. Su categorized the dragons that she found in many ways. Under Dr. Standish's direction Su made lists of distinctive features, proportions of body parts, derivations from other images and references and colors. Because she was a gifted artist and computer wizard, she rendered historical representations as "living" computer models for display on a high definition screen in her lab. So she had models of the dragon laying eggs, flying, walking on the land, swimming and settling in a cavern. When she reviewed these images with her professor, Dr. Standish began to see other relationships that brought new evidence to bear on their investigation.

Dr. Standish began to take interest in anything living that was associated with the word dragon in any language. She was particularly interested in the linkages of the dragon fly and the dragon tree, the latter being specific to the Canary Islands in the Eastern Atlantic Ocean. From the swimming image of the dragon, Dr. Standish deduced that the ancient nautical charts with pictures of sea serpents might be related, so she asked Su to find every sea serpent representation in the historical records and refine her image of the swimming dragon accordingly. From this method of pattern association, Su's computerized forms took new meaning. Now the professor and her student worked together to model the fossilized remains of the dragon bird to connect their most likely paths of mutation to produce the dragon models in Su's computer. In a flash of inspiration, Su asked her professor whether the feathers might be another key because the festival representations of dragons were covered with beautiful, iridescent colors, in fact all the colors of the rainbow, whose Greek name was Iris. Perhaps instead of scales, the student conjectured, the dragon's many colors were really derived from feathers. Dr. Standish was intrigued. She said that jungle birds with coloration most like the dragon representations should become part of the modeling exercises.

While Su began to trace three lines of evolution from the fossil remains—to the sea serpent, to the birds of paradise and to a land creature approximating the earliest representations in art, Dr. Standish began experimenting with computerized plastic molding devices by which she could transmit her findings in 3-D. Within three months she was able to create from Su's computer models plastic replications in the form of action figures that could be printed out in vivid, iridescent colors. She and Su studied the resultant action figures of the sea, air and land configurations, and they came to the conclusion that the three could, with very slight modifications, become a single configuration that walked on land, flew in the air and swam in the sea. The computer figures were modified accordingly, and the 3-D printer version of the result was exactly what Dr. Standish needed for her presentation at a symposium in Tokyo. The only trouble was that she needed the plastic version to be ten feet tall so that everyone could inspect it. She reasoned that the computer image could be distributed on disc to all attendees and be made available at her web site as well after her presentation. She called the coordinator of the symposium and told him of her requirement. She then sent him the 3-D computer rendering that Su had made. Dr. Parks said he would try to have the computer image printed so that the image was ten-feet high as she desired. He told her not to get her hopes up about the fidelity of the results to her computer rendering.

Dr. Standish and Su arrived at the symposium site a day early and discovered that the entire program had been re-oriented to center on her findings. Outside the doors of the building in which the symposium was to be held was a ten-foot replication of Su's computer image. It was beautiful because its feathers were tooled in a material that caused them to change color as you walked around the statue in the same way that hummingbird feathers change color as the bird moves through the air. The dragon bird's eyes seemed to follow Dr. Standish as she walked around the statue. In fact, the statue seemed to be alive. Dr. Standish had to place her hand on the surface of the feathers to reassure her that it was indeed a statue and not a living thing. Su said that she could not believe how well the manufacturers had done to bring out every detail in her computer image. Now finally she understood the power of her own rendering art.

The next afternoon to a most respectful, capacity audience Dr. Standish told the story of her project, giving due praise to Su for her rendering. On the twenty-one foot diagonal screen behind her was projected the computer image of the dragon bird that stood outside the building's entrance. The audience gasped as the computerized beast rose and flew and then dropped into the sea and swam. Finally the beast climbed out of the water, shook its feathers and looked around. When it saw an opening in the rocks, it entered a cavern where upon an enormous pile of gold it settled and slept. The image faded out and then became black. When Dr. Standish asked that the lights be turned on, an ovation rang out throughout the lecture hall. Scholars rushed down to the podium to give the paleontologist their business cards.

Three young Japanese men and one woman stood patiently by waiting for their chance to meet Dr. Standish. Su went up to them and bowed in the Japanese fashion. They bowed lower and handed her their business cards. They represented a major film studio, and they told Su they wanted to use the dragon bird as their monster in a full production animated film. They mentioned payment that would fund Dr. Standish's work for many years. Su suggested that they all meet for dinner after the symposium because she did not know when Dr. Standish was going to break free from her gawkers and admirers. They suggested a quiet restaurant and offered to pick up the tab if Dr. Standish and Su would come. They gave Su the address of the restaurant and departed. Two hours later Dr. Standish finished speaking with the last member of her audience who remained for questions. Dr. Standish and Su packed their things and strolled outside the symposium room in the direction of the glassed entrance to the building. There in the evening light they could see the enormous statue glistening. They stopped to admire their creation not because of the cast of the light but because of the way the light made the image double, as if two dragon birds were standing outside the building side by side. Su had the presence of mind to take a cell phone picture of the strange effect. Then the figure on the right turned its head and looked straight at Dr. Standish, spread its enormous wings and flew.

Su pressed her camera's automatic film button, but by that time the living dragon bird had flown. Dr. Standish ran out the door to catch a glimpse of where the creature was flying, and she saw it was heading straight into the sun. The dragon bird did not waver but continued on its trajectory until it was no longer visible. Looking around her, the professor saw that the area around the sculpture was empty. She and her assistant had been the only witnesses. Su came up to show her professor the one photograph that showed two identical figures standing side by side. The photograph might have been an optical illusion because in it was no indication that the second figure was alive. Being careful scholars, Dr. Standish and Su could not rule out that they had had a consensual hallucination, a wish fulfillment exercise that made their hypothesis real when actually nothing by way of a living dragon bird had really appeared. Still Dr. Standish knew what she had seen with her own eyes. Su was almost certain she had seen what her professor had seen. The two stunned women proceeded to meet the four filmmakers for dinner, resolving not to mention the odd appearance because it might lower their credibility.

Over sushi and sake the paleontologists and filmmakers talked terms for a movie tentatively titled, "Dragon Bird Battles Mothra." This would be the first, the filmmakers said, of a series of films featuring the Dragon Bird figure. The young filmmakers were sponsored by Sony, but their budget was limited. They said they could pay one million yen for the rights to reproduce the Dragon Bird computer imagery that Su had made. They could pay an additional royalty for each showing of the film in the domestic and international marketplace. Then additional royalties would accrue for syndication, digital release and action figures. Their ten-year projections showed amounts that made Dr. Standish and Su drop their jaws. The four entrepreneurs had thought everything through, and they had corporate lawyers draw up appropriate papers. They had even brought earnest money outside of contract terms as a bonus for immediate signing. Dr. Standish said that the contract would have to be revised to include her and Su as equals sharing the proceeds fifty-fifty. Su objected at her mentor's generosity, but Dr. Standish said that she deserved to be an equal partner in what lay ahead. The entrepreneurs said their lawyers would make adjustments to the contract while they all had more sake. That happened, and Dr. Standish and her assistant were able to sign electronically before they left the restaurant. A perfected copy of the signed document was in both women's respective in boxes when they returned to their hotel. The next morning before they left for the airport, they learned that their filmmakers had settled all their bills. They realized that Sony was a bountiful sponsor.

Meanwhile, as good scientists, the two women each documented her perceptions of the strange occurrence of the living dragon bird. When they compared them, their two accounts corresponded in every detail. If only, they thought, someone else had witnessed the breathtaking phenomenon. Why was it that in crowded Tokyo the area around the statue of the bird had been entirely vacant when the dragon bird landed and took off? What did it mean that the living bird had flow into the setting sun? What had lured the living bird to stand by the statue of itself?

Dr. Standish could not immediately answer these and a hundred other questions that rose in her mind. She did ask Su to examine every pixel of the cell-phone picture she had taken to determine any differences between the statue and the living dragon bird. She decided to do some calculations of where the flight line of the living dragon bird might have taken it. Clearly it had flown far into China, but where it finally landed along its course, she would have to discover by examining the route on GoogleEarth. She was convinced that the dragon bird had given her the key to finding it, just as she and Su had given the living bird the statue as a sign that humans were on its trail. Dr. Standish mused whether the crude human multi-person folk costumes of the dragon were purposed to be lures to bring the creature out from its hiding place. She asked Su to be on the lookout in her research for any references to figures of dragons used as enticements or lures for magical animals.

In the mean time, Su was joined in her lab by Miao the female filmmaker who had been at the dinner where the Sony contracts had been signed. Miao was excited to be working out the details of the Dragon Bird's movements while it fought the giant monster Mothra, which had battled against Godzilla and a handful of other Japanese monster figures. Miao was imaginative, but she was also a walking catalog of horror movies and an avid, amateur student of folklore. She was somewhat bored with doing yet another film about Mothra—her personal fourth in that line. Yes, the film would make lots of money, and Sony would be very happy. Yet Mothra was a purely mythical creature, the product of a comic-book mentality. In contrast, Miao wanted the dragon bird to have a worthy competitor that came out of the real imagination of East Asian people. She said she would like to see a battle between the dragon bird and the phoenix. That spontaneous suggestion hit a nerve with Su, who had independently traced one evolutionary path for the dragon bird to the phoenix. In Su's mind the two were not competitors but kindred, and she raised this objection with Miao.

"Su, do you come from a big family? I do not, but I know people in big families that fight all the time. Besides, the English have a myth of a lion and a unicorn fighting. And in Chinese tradition the dragon and the phoenix are sometimes shown as rampant equals in imperial embroidery artifacts."

"Miao, I know those artifacts. They are in my database. Do you mean to say that the dragon and the phoenix might have been rivals for imperial attention in China?"

"Why not? Chinese pit *tangban* warriors against *soban* merchants in society as shown in the configuration of the Forbidden City. Why not dragon and phoenix in myth? It's the same thing, in my judgment. Anyway, a fight between the dragon and the phoenix has never been done. The film would be fun to make if only I could imagine how the phoenix would maneuver while fighting the dragon bird!"

Su had a long discussion with Dr. Standish about the idea of the dragon and phoenix as both kindred and rivals both in naturalistic and mythic terms. The paleontologist listened attentively while Su recounted her research on the phoenix. Rather than redirect her protégé to focus exclusively on the dragon bird, the paleontologist okayed her pursuing a dual track, associating the dragon bird with the phoenix however possible. She told Su to make a 3-D computer model of the supposedly mythical phoenix so they both could compare the creatures in detail. The doctor told Su to start her modeling by returning to the evolutionary branch that led from the dragon bird fossil to the phoenix. That way, she was less likely to be influenced by the composite figure she had already made of the dragon bird.

It took Su fifteen days working almost nonstop to come up with her 3-D model of the phoenix. Miao was absolutely delighted because with it she could importune Sony to change characters and eliminate Mothra as the dragon bird's antagonist. Dr. Standish wanted a few modifications to Su's new model because some physiological mechanisms that Su had built into her computer figure could not possibly work in the real world. It was clear to both the professor and her student as the phoenix figure evolved in the computer environment that it was a different species from the dragon bird entirely. The more it differentiated, the more it took on characteristics that were radically altered from its kin. For example, the phoenix could never have been a sea creature, and it would have been uncomfortable living on the land or in a cavern. Second, if the phoenix had ever lived in nature, no fossilized remains had been discovered to support that hypothesis. Yet fossilized remains would have been difficult for reasons yet to be disclosed. Third, the mythology surrounding the phoenix indicated a cycle of death in flames and rebirth from an egg laid in the ashes of the immolated parent bird. That cycle would explain the absence of fossilized remains except that some eggs might have survived but had not yet been uncovered.

Miao was intrigued rather than put off by these scientific considerations. She was wholly convinced that the phoenix could supplant Mothra as the competitive rival to the dragon bird. She immediately began working up sketches for the filmic internecine battle between the dragon bird and the phoenix. She saw the immolation of the phoenix as its best defense while the dragon bird could escape the phoenix's wrath by entering the water or hiding in a cave. Perhaps the dragon bird could take revenge on the phoenix by crushing its egg after the incineration, but only if the egg could be found in the smoldering ashes of its parent. Su worked with Miao to get the tenets for the fight put down in writing, and she ran five different scenarios in which the two animals fought against each other in her computer. Miao watched these scenarios entranced with what they suggested for transposition to the big screen. She took the 3-D scenarios to Tokyo to share with her counterparts.

Dr. Standish meanwhile had used GoogleEarth to define the path that the living dragon bird had taken on its flight into China. Although it might have landed anywhere, she thought it likely that the dragon bird landed somewhere in Liaoning where the fossilized remains of its ancestors had lain. She mused that generations of spiders spun their webs on the same location for generations. Why shouldn't the dragon birds do the same? Since the paleontologist was both creative and a good listener, she asked Su to do research on all the latest paleontological finds in Liaoning. She was looking for eggs that had not been identified as belonging to a specific, known dinosaur. Something about the story that Miao had decided to tell gave her the odd feeling that art had imitated life. What if the two symbolic creatures actually did coexist as brother developments in a long, natural process and eventually came into competitive collision that remained in the collective human consciousness as a compelling myth. Usually, she reasoned, myths came about because they explained the otherwise unexplainable. They sometimes also conformed to observables like the ice queen.

Su found in her investigations that at least forty dozen fossilized dinosaur eggs had been discovered in digs all over Liaoning. Except for two eggs they were regular in shape and size. The two exceptions were larger and more symmetrical. They had been found in isolation where most of the other egg fossils had been found in groups of six or more. The two eggs showed evidence of having experienced extreme heat as in an oven. Their surfaces were like porcelain. These two unusual eggs were now in a glass case in a natural history museum in Liaoning. Su asked her major professor whether she should take a close look at the two eggs to determine whether they might be phoenix eggs. Dr. Standish told her that they were both going to Liaoning to look for the cavern of the dragon bird, so they could both drop by the museum and take a look at the eggs while they were in the area.

Fortunately from Sony's advance against royalties for the film, the two paleontologists had enough money to make the trip to China and mount their land expedition in Liaoning. There they were met by the four young filmmaker entrepreneurs and a large film crew with all kinds of filmmaking equipment. When Sony had found out from Miao that the paleontology trip had been scheduled, executives arranged for a trip to Liaoning for the whole crew. Miao had prevailed: the film that was now titled, "The Dragon Bird Battles the Phoenix." The film company would use the natural background of the province in their movie, and they arranged to see the two "phoenix eggs" that were displayed with signage proclaiming the same message in the museum of natural history.

Instead of a single jeep in the vast yellow wilderness, a caravan of a single jeep followed by fifteen Sony film vehicles set out along the path that GoogleEarth had provided as the most likely route of the living dragon bird. Their immediate objective was a rocky region that was known to be so full of caves that troglodytes had lived there as long as human memory. Through the director of the natural history museum, Dr. Standish had arranged to meet an elder who lived there who knew the caves well. He would be her guide as she searched the area for what she was looking for.

"Dr. Standish, I presume," the elder said. "I am Xiaolong Ma Chi. Please call me Chi. I understand from the director that you are looking for large birds that live in caves. Many large birds live in the crevices and caves among the rock formations that you see, and there are also many bats that live in the large caverns deep in the mountain and underground. Can you tell me anything specific about what you are looking for?"

"Chi, I'm afraid I'll only know what I am looking for when I see it. Can you tell me whether there is any folklore about birds or dragons among the people who live here?"

"Doctor, at every Chinese New Year the ritual of the dragon and the phoenix must be reenacted on the plain below the mountain."

"Excuse me, did you say, 'reenacted.'"

"Yes, it is the reenactment of the great battle in antiquity between the dragon and the phoenix. It is because of this battle that the earliest emperor of China took the two figures as his emblem." This aroused the curiosity of both the doctor and her protégé, but Miao and her people looked at one another with amazement.

"What is the story of the dragon and the phoenix?" Su asked.

The elder replied as follows:

In ancient times a dragon and a phoenix both lived in these mountains. According to legend the dragon guarded a hoard of gold in an enormous cavern deep within the mountain. The phoenix stayed mostly by itself and lived off what it captured on the plains. Its gift was good fortune, and it sought renewal through periodic self immolation.

One day a great sage came to ask which of the two—the dragon or the phoenix—offered the greater gift for humans.

The dragon showed the sage its golden hoard and asked, "What could be more valuable to humans than wealth? Men fought for gold and coveted what I the dragon gathered and guarded."

The phoenix took umbrage with what the dragon said. She told the sage to witness the gift of eternal life, saying, "Why do men need gold if they are going to die eventually? They could not take the gold with them into death. Contrariwise, if men had eternal life, they would be immortal and could have and keep as much gold as they wanted forever."

When the dragon heard what the phoenix said, it was enraged and would not permit the phoenix to demonstrate its power. Instead it attacked at once, and the phoenix was forced to defend itself. The sage stood back and watched the heroic battle of creatures that knew how to fight fiercely and kill their prey with finesse as well as strength.

The battle went on for three days. The first day put the contest on the land where the figures seemed well matched as equals. The second day put them in the air where they fought with the same tactics with their wings, rapacious mouths and claws, and reached a draw. Finally on the third day the dragon made its way to the water and slipped beneath the waves, raising its head only to taunt the phoenix to continue the fight there.

The phoenix saw its opportunity and turned to the sage and spread its wings in a bowing motion. It then suddenly and spontaneously burst into flames that burned with such heat that they singed the hair from the crown and eyebrows of the sage. The dragon, furious that the phoenix had resorted to this stratagem, told the sage that it had won the contest and the cowardly phoenix had reneged and forfeited.

The sage nodded as if in agreement with the dragon, but he withdrew to the mountain top and sat cross-legged in a holy trance contemplating for a full week without eating or drinking. At the end of that time, the sage came down from the mountain and carefully raked through the ashes of the phoenix looking for something. He found an egg that appeared to be made of porcelain. He carefully picked up the egg and wrapped it in his robe. Then he went away to continue his quest for truth.

Many years later the emperor heard the story of the battle of the dragon and the phoenix from a disciple of the sage. The emperor asked the disciple whether the sage had discovered the truth he was looking for. With gay eyes the disciple opened his robe and gave the emperor the broken halves of the shell of the egg of the phoenix. "Here," the disciple said, " is the proof that the phoenix lives. Where is the hoard of gold that the dragon guards?"

The emperor from that time forward fashioned his emblem with both the dragon and the phoenix on it. He explained that an emperor must hoard gold for his people, but he must also perpetuate the imperial rule. Though the two were opposite goals, he said, only the two together would provide harmony and perpetuity for the people of China.

The elder made an impression on both the paleontologists and the filmmakers. The latter now had a story within which they could place the heroic battle that lay at the center of their filmic vision. How much they could make of the sage and the moral dimensions of the story, they just did not know. While the elder escorted the paleontologists through the cave complex on the mountain, the filmmakers shot footage of the mountain and the surroundings and resolved to shoot footage in the East China Sea to fill out their settings for the drama. They figured they would create the great cavern of the dragon with its hoard of gold on their computers just as they would manufacture the timeless battle between the dragon and the phoenix. They were so wrapped up in their photography that they lost track of the time. That night they camped out under the stars, and the two chief photographers shot footage at dusk and at dawn to flesh out their background studies.

Meanwhile Dr. Standish and Su were led deeper and deeper into the mountain, the guide leading with an electric torch. They wound through narrow openings as they descended until at midnight they were in a deep underground cavern that could have held a large village, only it was filled with heaps of gold in the form of gold dust, nuggets, roseate quartz ore beaded with gold, gold bars and coins. On top of this hoard sat an enormous dragon bird that eyed its hoard jealously and then rose and flapped its wings and hissed at the three intruders.

"This bird only attacks those who love gold. Fortunately, we three have no greed for what it protects, and it knows this. Touch nothing and keep your eyes averted from its eyes. You'll notice that there on the pile of gold that looks like a nest made of gold dust lies a porcelain egg. That is the egg of a phoenix, which the dragon now guards as jealously as its gold. They are related, the dragon bird and the phoenix, so they don't always fight. I think the dragon bird is unhappy when the phoenix decides to start another cycle because it has no playmate that understands him."

Su asked, "So is the dragon male and the phoenix female?"

The elder answered, "It is the yang, and the phoenix is the yin. Together they make one whole vision. This is very Chinese."

"So what do we do now that we have witnessed this priceless vision?"

"Say nothing about what you have seen. What could be

gained by that except misery and ruin? Help make the film that tells the story because that is what counts after all. The coelacanth is one thing, the dragon bird is another. Oh, yes, professor, your reputation precedes you. We may be troglodytes, but we are intellectuals of a fashion too."

"And, I would guess, you are the descendants of the disciple that spoke with the earliest emperor. Is that true?" The professor was connecting everything she had learned, and the elder was   impressed.

"We of this mountain are descended both from the disciple and the emperor through the emperor's youngest daughter who refused to be confined in the Forbidden City. She escaped and, with the disciple's help, came here. They had a family far from the imperial court and all the insidious designs of evil men and women. Here the couple had all the gold in the world, but they did not desire it. Instead they had love and understanding among each other and two pet creatures that defined everything they both hated in society. I could show you their tombs, but we have to be ascending now or our torches' batteries will fail. Your friends will be looking for you after daylight, and they may take a wrong path that leads them here. I do not think the dragon bird would like that."

"I have one more question before we ascend. What made the dragon bird come to Tokyo to be with the statue figure we had made of him?"

"That I cannot tell you. Are you certain that this dragon bird came to Tokyo and not some other?"

The elder then turned and retraced his steps, and the paleontologists followed him through the rest of the night. They emerged at sunrise and saw that the skies were black with birds of all kinds, dipping and wheeling and singing in the morning air. The elder returned to his family and the paleontologists returned to their caravan, which was now packed and ready to retrace its path.

Miao said, "We've got the pictures we came for. The finishing touch was the footage of the birds in the morning. Wow. What an opportunity! In all your wanderings through the caves in the mountain, did you see anything interesting?"

Su said, "Nothing surprising, and nothing to write home about. The elder told us some more stories, but the one you heard before we descended was the essence of it all."

Dr. Standish said, "It's time we all got back to write an article about our findings. I don't think, however, that we'll be able to place it in a paleontological journal. Perhaps a journal of folklore? Anyway, right now we have a contract to help with a film whose statement will not need much scholarly interpretation—unless we have to interpret the sage's comments for the general audience."

Miao said, "Don't worry. Some things should remain a mystery to maintain the interest. After all, we must think of the sequels. And perhaps a whole new movie about the phoenix should be made. I don't like the idea but my associates are enthralled with something they are tentatively titling, 'The Phoenix Battles Mothra.' I'm okay with another line, but I'm thinking, 'Dragon Bird of Liaoning.' The premise is that two paleontologists went deep into a mountain and found a dragon bird on top of piles of gold. You two would be the heroines, and the elder would be a latter day sage. What do you think of that? So you don't like it—I can tell from your expressions. Forget it. I take it back. Give me some slack. Just because you came up with nothing, you don't have to be cross with me. Do you want a Snickers bar? I've got two extras. Okay, then. After all, you must be starved. All night walking around in a cave in the dark—and for what?"

***

ABOUT THE JUDGES

CLARE WALLACE

Clare graduated with a BA in Creative Writing and Cultural Studies at Bath Spa University, and went on to gain a distinction on the MA in Creative Writing. Having worked earlier with Luxton Harris Ltd literary agency, she is currently the Head of Rights and Literary Agent with Darley Anderson, and is scouting for new talent in commercial and accessible literary general fiction and all types of women's fiction. Clare is also building the children's list and is looking for new children's authors and illustrators.

At the Agency Clare represents authors both in the UK and the US including Kerry Fisher, Rosie Blake, Martyn Ford, Cesca Major, Kim Slater, Polly Ho-Yen, Dave Rudden, Beth Reekles, Caroline Crowe and Adam Perrott and illustrators Jon Holder, Clare Mackie, Loretta Schauer and Lorna Scobie.

BRETT ALAN SANDERS

Brett is a writer, translator, and recently retired teacher living in Tell City, Indiana. He earned a BA in Spanish (with an English minor) from Indiana University and an MALS at the University of Southern Indiana. He has been a contributing writer at Tertulia Magazine where for "Tertullian's Blog" he wrote the occasional column "Arte Retórica," and a former columnist for the Perry County (IN) News. In addition he served a brief stint as managing editor at New Works Review and has translated for the literary-arts website Suelta. He has published original essays, fiction, and literary translations in a variety of journals including Hunger Mountain, Artful Dodge, The Antigonish Review, *Confluence: The Journal of Graduate Liberal Studies*, and Rosebud. He has also published a YA novella (A Bride Called Freedom, Ediciones Nuevo Espacio, 2003) and two book-length translations from the work of Buenos Aires writer *María Rosa Lojo* (Awaiting the Green Morning, Host Publications, 2008; Passionate Nomads, Aliform Publications, 2011).

www.brettalansanders.wordpress.com

ANISHA BHADURI

Anisha has spent more than a decade in journalism. In 2012, her first published work of fiction featured in the Random House title 'She Writes: A collection of Short Stories'. Following a decade-long stint with *The Statesman* in India, she is currently deputy chief editor at *China Daily* in Hong Kong. The first Indian woman to become a *Konrad Adenauer Stiftung* Fellow, she was a visiting faculty to the Statesman Print Journalism School, Kolkata for nearly five years. In 2009, Anisha won the first prize in a national literary contest for women writers organized by the British Council in India. In December, 2011, she was conferred the Pradyot Bhadra Young Journalist Award for Excellence by Pracheen Kala Kendra. In 2013 Anisha was one of the judges for the Love on The Road short story competition hosted by Malinki Press.

LEELA DEVI PANIKAR

Leela Devi Panikar is a fiction writer and photographer. After spending many years in Malaysia, Wales and Vietnam, she has settled in Hong Kong. Her extensive travel and various cultural experiences are portrayed in her two published short story collections: Bathing Elephants & Floating Petals. She has been awarded for her writing by the BBC (UK); Turner Maxwell (UK); and The South China Morning Post and Radio Television, Hong Kong. Her third short-story collection Phantom Visitor is to be published soon and she has two novels in the making. Her articles and stories have been published in journals and periodicals in Hong Kong and overseas.

Website - www.leela.net

Email - leela@leela.net

ABOUT THE EDITOR

Anirban Ray Choudhury co-founded and was for over a decade the editor of the Quill & Ink, a webzine devoted to the arts. He was also a columnist for the online knowledge portal www.buzzle.com writing on a variety of subjects, ranging from literature to science. A published poet in both online and offline media, he had helped set up Pen Himalaya, one of the first webzines for poets and writers from Nepal. He is actively engaged in several literary projects, and is the guest editor for the Hourglass Literary Magazine from Bosnia.

A finance professional from India, Anirban currently lives with his journalist wife and school going son in Hong Kong, where he prefers to take his breaks from the perpetual monotony of juggling with digits and numbers by delving into football, literature and the arts (though not necessarily in that order).